VERA'S VALOUR

Vera's life, as a wartime bride and British Restaurant cook, is thrown into turmoil when she is handed a vitally important message for her Royal Engineer husband — just after he has departed for D-Day preparations. She eventually catches up with him, but danger is all around them and she must find her own way home again, leaving Geoff to his duties — and without having given him an important message of her own . . .

Books by Anne Holman
in the Linford Romance Library:

SAIL AWAY TO LOVE
HER HEART'S DESIRE
FLYING TO HEAVEN
FINDING LOVE
HIDDEN LOVE
SECRET LOVE
CAPTURED LOVE
THE LONGMAN GIRL
THE OWNER OF THORPE HALL
THE CAPTAIN'S MESSENGER
BELLE OF THE BALL
CASSIE'S FAVOUR
THE GOLDEN DOLLY
A NEW LIFE FOR ROSEMARY
VERA'S VICTORY
FOLLIES HOTEL

ANNE HOLMAN

VERA'S VALOUR

Complete and Unabridged

LINFORD
Leicester

First published in Great Britain in 2010

First Linford Edition
published 2011

British Library CIP Data

Holman, Anne, *1934 –*
  Vera's valour. - -
  (Linford romance library)
  1. World War, *1939 – 1945*- -Social aspects- -
  Great Britain- -Fiction. 2. Women cooks- -
  Fiction. 3. Great Britain. Army. Royal
  Engineers- -Fiction. 4. Love stories.
  5. Large type books.
  I. Title II. Series
  823.9'2–dc22

  ISBN 978–1–44480–527–7

Published by
F. A. Thorpe (Publishing)
Anstey, Leicestershire

Set by Words & Graphics Ltd.
Anstey, Leicestershire
Printed and bound in Great Britain by
T. J. International Ltd., Padstow, Cornwall

This book is printed on acid-free paper

Vera Doesn't Get To Say Goodbye

1944

Vera was almost in tears by the time she parked the car outside her mother's house in the Norfolk town of Lynn. She wiped the wetness from under her eyes with her fingertips, and took several deep breaths before she got out of the car.

'Come on, out you get,' she instructed the two dogs in the back of the car to jump down on to the pavement. After grabbing her suitcase, as well as the dog leads, she walked towards the house.

'Hello, dear!' her mother called from the back garden where she was unpegging dry clothes from the washing line.

When the dogs barked and began to

1

tug on their leads, Vera pulled them back sharply, saying, 'Hey, you two must behave, or Mum will have to put you both into kennels — and you won't like that.'

Mrs Carter was in her apron as she waddled towards the gate saying, 'My goodness. Two dogs, and a suitcase — are you moving back home?'

'Mum I've come to ask you . . . '

At that point Vera couldn't prevent the tears from streaming down her cheeks.

'Goodness me! Whatever's happened?' Frowning as she clicked open the gate, Mrs Carter rushed to comfort her daughter, aware that wartime brought disasters. 'Come into the house and tell me all about it. We'll take the leads off the dogs and let them run in the garden — they'll be quite safe there.'

Having released the dogs, Vera was ushered into the kitchen by her mother who asked her, 'Now what's upset you?'

Vera sat down heavily on a wooden kitchen chair and putting her arms on the scrubbed kitchen table did just what she had been struggling not to do — she had a good cry.

Mrs Carter put the kettle on and a little later a cup of tea was placed before Vera, and as she sipped the hot tea it revived her.

'Now start at the beginning,' her mother said, eyeing her suitcase. 'Have you had a row and left Geoff?'

'He's the one who's gone,' said Vera, holding her teacup.

'Dear me. Why?'

Vera gave a shuddering sigh.

'His war work. He left a message. I saw it when I came home from work this evening.'

'So, what's new? He's often had to go away with his engineering work. He's been helping to construct those artificial harbours for D-Day, hasn't he?'

Vera clattered her cup down into the saucer as she hissed, 'Shush! It's top secret.'

'I know it is. But I don't pretend to know anything about it — only what

3

I've heard you and Geoff mention on occasions.'

Vera stretched over to pat her mother's hand.

'I know you don't gossip, Mum, but Geoff has said time and time again that it is an enormous engineering project. He has to oversee hundreds of dockworkers, and factory workers, who've been making it — and they must all keep it a secret. The enemy must not get wind of it — or it could mean the invasion will not succeed. It is as serious as that.'

Mrs Carter nodded. 'I know Geoff has been worried about it.'

'Worried? He's been a pain in the neck, bad tempered, and inconsiderate. His papers are strewn all over the house. He forgets I have an exacting job of work to do, too. It's horrible coming home tired out after work and finding the house in a mess day after day.'

'Some men are very untidy.'

'Untidy? It's not just that he's been untidy — he's been unbearable to live with! I wouldn't have married him if I'd known he was going to be like that.'

Mrs Carter was silent as she looked at Vera sympathetically.

'I don't suppose he means to be difficult, Vera. He's a high-ranking officer with an enormous amount of vital war work occupying his mind. That's what's made him anxious and short-tempered. And if he gets orders to move to another place he has to go. It must be just as hard on him as it is on you.'

'I know,' Vera said miserably, remembering how her husband had told her that as a young officer he'd made a mistake with constructing a temporary bridge, and a soldier had been killed.

'He's terrified of making another mistake — although he's a skilled and inventive engineer, and valued by the army. And I knew they'd given him a tremendous responsibility assisting with the construction of Mulberry — that's the codename of the huge floating docks needed to give the army supplies after they've landed in France.'

Vera stopped talking and sighed. Although she was only twenty-two years old, she'd been given a huge responsibility too, as organiser of several British Restaurants in the area.

Feeding hundreds of hungry people in wartime with very little food available took all her ingenuity. And, although she was trained as a Cordon Bleu Chef, some of the cooks and assistants didn't even know how to boil a potato correctly before she trained them. But it was no good complaining — in wartime you just had to make the best of things.

Having a sense of humour helped, and Vera bucked up after talking to her mother about her worries.

'Yes, Mum,' she nodded, 'we've both been working hard and are feeling exhausted. This war has made everyone feel tired. Still, sometimes I feel I can't go on living with a man who is married to a floating dock!'

Mrs Carter smiled a little as she

poured them a second cup of tea. 'If I didn't know you were a sensible girl, and have been working so hard yourself, I would say you were overreacting — but I believe that there's more reason than him ignoring you, and his bad temper that's made you come here this evening.'

There was, of course, but Vera didn't quite know how best to explain it.

Not hearing a reply to her question, Mrs Carter stirred some sugar into her cup of tea.

Vera was thinking how she'd had to say goodbye to her first boyfriend, and he'd then been killed in Malta. She shuddered to think of what might happen to Geoff. Would she ever see him again?

At last she explained, 'Geoff's had to go, as you said. But as I was at work all day, I wasn't able to see him off . . . it's terrible not to have been able to say goodbye . . . and wish him well. And not know what might happen to him . . . '

It hurt Vera because, despite her grumbles about Geoff, she loved him deeply. But she wondered why he hadn't left an affectionate message for her — had his engineering work engulfed him so much he no longer loved her?

She sniffed and tried not to break down again.

'Lots of lovers have to part in wartime,' her mother reminded her.

Vera felt a flash of anger. As if that helped to know that other people suffered from being parted too!

Mother and daughter looked at each other and Vera's moment of crossness evaporated. She knew she was lucky to have an understanding mother — especially as she had to ask her a favour.

'It is true I didn't come here just to tell you my woes. I know you have your worries too, Mum. The truth is I've come to ask you to look after our dogs for a while.'

'Can't you manage them?'

'Yes, normally I can. But I have to go away too.'

Mrs Carter stiffened.

'Oh? How long for?'

'Hopefully, only for a few days.'

Mrs Carter shifted herself to sit more comfortably on her chair. 'Now tell me the truth. I want to know what all this is about, Vera.'

Vera explained in a rush.

'Geoff left before a messenger came on a motorbike with some secret papers for him. Now I must track him down to give them to him.'

'Why couldn't the messenger find him?'

'He didn't know where he was.'

'Do you know where he's gone?'

'Not exactly, Mum.'

'So how will you get the papers to him?'

'I'll have to go to the local army camp and ask for him.' She didn't add that she feared he wouldn't be there, but they might know where he was.

'Can't you telephone the camp?'

Vera shook her head.

'Even if he's there, he'll need the papers.'

'Perhaps he won't.'

Vera put her fingers through her hair.

'But say he does? And people's lives depended on it?'

Mrs Carter gave a little shiver.

'Aren't the army planning to attack the Germans in France very soon?'

'That's the point, Mum. They are. I've heard it may begin any day now. And it's such vital work Geoff has to do. I can't presume that what's been sent to him is unimportant — and he can do without it, can I? I just don't know. All I know is that parts of Mulberry are going to be assembled somewhere on the South Coast very soon. And then the huge docks are going to be towed across the Channel to France.

'Geoff is involved with some aspect of that job. He's like an overseer to make sure the operation works. He has the expertise, but he too depends on the co-operation and skill of others. And I know he must be worried sick about casualties after the previous attempt was a disaster . . . and the weather forecast is awful . . . '

'Now calm yourself, Vera. You didn't give him the job — the army did. You couldn't have stopped him from going to do his job — even if you'd wanted to. Geoff has a dangerous job to do like every soldier in this coming conflict. Just go back home and wait for him to return.'

Vera gave a loud wail.

'I'd like to, Mum. But I can't when I believe the information in this military pouch may be needed to do his part of the job. Why do you think they sent a messenger and didn't just ring him?'

Mrs Carter put her head to one side, saying, 'I expect he's working with other men who know what has to be done.'

'I don't think they know as much as Geoff does about his part of the work. He designed and had made essential parts of the harbour. It's like doing a huge jigsaw. If he can't do his part properly, because he's left some important instructions behind — '

'Oh dear!' Mrs Carter's eyes widened as she looked at Vera.

'So you see, I must go after Geoff with this pouch. That's why I'm here, to ask you to look after the dogs. I've got their beds and dog dishes and some food for them in the back of the car.'

Her mother could see it would be no use arguing with Vera. Once her daughter dug her heels in, Vera could be the most stubborn creature on earth, so she said, 'Well, if you feel you must. You'd better go. It's no great problem for me to look after the dogs. John Baxter always takes his dog for a walk every day, so I'll ask him if I can join him. My worry will be you chasing about looking for Geoff. Are you sure it is necessary?'

'I believe it is, Mum. Only he will know, when I find him, if my journey was really necessary.'

Mrs Carter smiled at Vera quoting the well-known wartime government slogan — 'Is your journey really necessary?' Giving a sigh, she stood up scraping the wooden chair legs on the kitchen floor, 'Well if you are set on it I suppose you must go. But what about your job?'

'I rang Margaret. She knows enough to take over while I'm away.'

Mrs Carter hid a tear as she walked over to the kitchen sink with the empty cups, saying, 'Very well, get in the car and beetle off to the army camp. I'll have an evening meal ready for you when you get back.'

Vera replied, 'Mum, I may not be back this evening. And I'm not taking the car. I'm going to take my bike from the shed and put some of my clothes in a rucksack so I can take them with me.'

Vera Sets Out To Help

As the evening sky became dark with clouds Vera cycled along the straight flat road towards the camp. The gusty wind blew up across the Fenlands with a viciousness that made her bicycle wobble, making her think she was going to be swept off the road into the black earth fields either side of it at any moment.

Occasionally droning aircraft came far too low for comfort over her head. She began to think she was foolish not to have taken the car, but petrol was very scarce in wartime, and rationed, and she was only allowed a certain amount to do her job.

Anyway, the other reason she chose to ride her bike was because she wanted to be able to get from one area of the camp to another — and she knew, because she had to sometime visit them, how

14

vast the military camps were.

But her old bike had been stuck in Mum's garden shed during the year she'd been married because she didn't need it at the farm cottage where she and Geoff lived. And the way the pedals were cranking reminded her that she should have oiled it.

She heard a car coming behind her and was furious when a jeep raced by almost knocking her off her bike. Wobbling to become straight on the road again, Vera felt annoyed to realise the pedal shaft had scratched her leg, resulting in a ladder up her stocking.

She spoke angrily to the jeep racing off ahead of her.

The invasion might be taking place soon, but there's no point in killing people before you have to — or laddering their stockings!

Then she realised that in the fading light the jeep may not have seen her and she should have put on her bicycle lights. But she couldn't because they weren't working as she needed new batteries.

By the time she'd arrived at the camp's sentry box, Vera felt like turning around and going back to Mum's for the evening meal she'd been told was being cooked for her.

'I'd like to speak to Colonel Parkington. Urgently,' she told the hard faced military policeman standing with a rifle at the gate.

'The camp ain't entertaining ladies tonight, miss. There's no weekly camp dance, only an army exercise that's had everyone dancing about all day.'

'Ha, ha, very funny! Now listen. I'm Colonel Parkington's wife and I must see him.' Vera produced her identity card and the official looking pouch from her bicycle basket and held it up for the soldier to see.

'Sarge!' bellowed the sentry over his shoulder, 'Come 'ere will yer?'

The sergeant came out of the guardhouse and blinked at her. 'Blimey! It's Mrs Parkington, isn't it?'

'It is. I need to speak to my husband. It's important.'

'Well, ma'am, I don't know where you'll find him. The camp's been like a busy ant hill all day with soldiers and vehicles coming and going.'

'Just ring the Camp Commander's office and say I'm here if you please, sergeant.'

'Yes, ma'am.'

She heard the sergeant's boots as he crunched away into an inner room, then she overheard him give the order, 'Jock, ring the Commander's office and say Parkie's missus is here with an important message for him.'

After a few minutes the sergeant came back to her.

'Sorry, ma'am. Colonel Parkington left the camp a few hours ago.'

Vera frowned. 'Where did he go?'

'Not allowed to say, ma'am, even if I knew.'

'Well, let me talk to someone who will be able to tell me.'

'There's been a lot going on all day.' He tapped his nose. 'Everyone's preparing for the invasion.'

17

Vera almost stamped her foot as she raised her voice.

'That's exactly why my husband may want this pouch, sergeant. I must get it to him.'

'If you give it to me, I'll do my best to see he gets it.'

Vera huffed, 'I must give it to him myself. That way I'll know he'll get it as soon as possible.'

The sergeant could see she meant business, and said, 'OK. Ride up the road ahead, turn right and you'll see the sign to the Commander's office. And may I suggest you put your bicycle lamps on, Mrs Parkington?'

Vera thanked him, but ignored his warning about her bicycle lights because what could she do to put them on until she could buy some batteries?

★   ★   ★

The whole camp seemed strangely deserted. Soon she was explaining to an army secretary why she'd come. He was

18

a courteous older soldier, no doubt a volunteer, who told her, 'Colonel Parkington left here at around four this afternoon, ma'am.'

'And where is he now?'

'On the way to the south coast, I should imagine.'

Vera scowled at him.

'Forget your imagination. I want to know the facts. You can see this pouch has *Top Secret*, clearly printed on it. Colonel Parkington needs to have it as soon as possible.'

'Leave it with me. I'll see he gets it.'

'If I leave it with your imagination he may get it by Christmas. He needs it now. Please get on the phone and find out where he is.'

The bespectacled secretary looked offended as he said, 'Sit down, ma'am. I'll see what I can find out.'

Vera was about to say, don't take all day about it, when she realised the lights were on in the Nissen hut, and the windows looked black. Outside the daylight was going. The day was over.

But her search for Geoff wasn't. That, she realised, had only just begun.

He rang several numbers asking for Geoff's whereabouts and it was after awhile he said to Vera, 'I've been told Colonel Parkington's on his way to Selsey.'

'Selsey? Where's that? I suppose I'll have to get there.'

'Come and look at this map. Selsey's near Chichester, in Sussex. It'll be a long way for you to ride your bike!'

Somehow this flippant remark made Vera's blood boil.

'Oh, I'll get there. And I'll find him,' she retorted.

Surprised by her vehemence, the secretary said, as if anxious to get rid of her, 'Try the transport station. They may have a truck going there.'

But, a little later, when Vera approached the huge hangar, usually crammed full of vehicles, it was empty. No sign of anyone.

'Hello, are you lost?'

Hearing a young woman's voice, Vera

swung around to see a couple of young uniformed girls approaching her.

'Yes,' Vera admitted, 'I need transport to Selsey, and there doesn't seem to be a car or truck anywhere on the camp.'

The girls looked at each other. One said, 'Everyone left today — except us.'

'You mean there's no way I can get to there?'

The girls looked at each other again.

'Well, we're going tomorrow morning. We're going to drive a NAAFI van.'

Vera brightened.

'Can I go with you?'

'How do we know you are not a German spy?'

Vera smiled and took out her military identity card she used when she had to visit military camps for her work.

'I'm Vera Parkington, Colonel Parkington's wife, and I have something I must give him.'

The girls smiled.

'Oooh! So you're Parkie's wife are you? He's a real heart-throb.'

Not, thought Vera, all the time! But

she smiled thinking of her beloved husband.

Then the girls relaxed. One said, 'I'm Susie Salter and she's Doreen Thornhill. We're NAAFI girls.'

Vera then remembered their uniforms, and smiled broadly.

'We are like sisters,' she said determined to be friendly, 'because I do similar work — providing meals for people who come to the British Restaurants.'

The ice was broken between them and for Vera it was a great relief to find two young women like herself who soon understood her problem — the necessity of getting the message to Colonel Parkington as soon as possible.

They were soon walking over to the NAAFI canteen and there Vera ate a plateful of sausage and mash and they were able to discuss how they were going to smuggle her down to Selsey, because, as Susie put it, 'Our manageress, Dulcie Swanton, is a right tartar. She might not let you thumb a lift with us. She'd frighten Hitler!'

Vera just hoped she wouldn't meet this dreadful manageress, Dulcie Swanton — although, Vera herself was quite capable of sending shivers down many people's backs.

The Journey Begins

'What's the name of this engineering wizard we're supposed to be picking up?'

The SOE soldier with his rifle at the ready, and lying on his belly in a Normandy field late at night, replied, 'Colonel Parkington.'

His companion whistled.

'He'll need to be a wizard with this French coast crawling with Germans. What's his mission?'

'Believe it or not, Churchill dreamed up the idea of the invasion troops bringing their own harbour with them — a floating dock, and they're going to put the ruddy thing somewhere along this coast so they can get the supplies in after the invasion troops are ashore.'

'Whew! Dream on.'

'Well this Parkington fella thinks it's possible, that's why he's coming to wave the thing into place.'

'If he lives to see it.'

'If any of us live to see it. The whole invasion seems dicey to me.'

The two soldiers' attention was taken up with the sound of a low flying aircraft and soon three parachutes could be seen floating down to earth. Trained in special services work, the two soldiers quickly made their way to the drop zone, and in a short time were able to locate the men who'd been flown into France from an airfield in England.

Hurrying the new arrivals to a nearby village and a safe house, they left the Royal Engineers with some agents.

Colonel Geoff Parkington was visibly shaken after his first parachute jump, and required some brandy kindly offered by the French agents to help him recover.

'I wouldn't feel quite so apprehensive about this massive project if I had the papers I was told were going to be sent to me before I left,' he told his second in command.

'Geoff, you'll see to it the job's done OK, I know you'll get around any problems we face.'

Geoff Parkington groaned quietly. He was frankly, scared. The huge floating dock was going to be on its way soon after the invasion took place. He'd used up all his courage to make himself do the parachute jump — and still felt wobbly after doing it. He was haunted by a past mistake in an engineering job, which had cost a soldier his life. He had a bad cold, and the weather was atrocious — rain, rain, rain. Would it ever stop?

The French coast was well defended by the Germans — and they were excellent fighters — and soon the RAF would be dropping bombs everywhere.

The chance of being killed or injured was . . . well, he didn't like to think of the likelihood of it. And deep in his heart he regretted he hadn't been able to bid his beloved wife, Vera, goodbye, because he'd had to hurry away immediately when he'd been ordered to go to France and prepare the Mulberry B dock landing area.

The only comfort he could think of was that British engineers had done a brilliant job, making Mulberry, and it should work as well as Churchill had foreseen. And Vera was a courageous lady who would not go to pieces when she learned that he had gone off to France to help with the invasion.

Geoff Parkington smiled as he envisaged Vera sitting comfortably in her armchair in the cottage with a cup of tea in her hands, and their two dogs snoozing by her feet. And he hoped she would forgive him for his bad temper over the past few months when he'd been working so hard on Mulberry.

★   ★   ★

Actually, Vera was far from their cottage, and dogs — and from being comfortable, as she tried to sleep on a makeshift bed the NAAFI girls had rigged up for her in their little hut.

27

Nevertheless, she did sleep eventually and was woken by Susie offering her a cup of tea.

'Rise and shine, ducky. We'll be on our way soon.'

Stiff, and feeling unwilling to go anywhere except back home, Vera gulped down the tea, and after visiting the wash room she scrambled into her clothes.

She found the two NAAFI girls ready for her to be boarded into the back of the mobile canteen.

Soon she was being trundled in the van out of the camp and starting the long drive down to the south coast.

Hours of being seated on the floor of the van, with her bicycle propped up by her, was not a comfortable time for Vera, who was shunted about as the van stopped and swerved and sometimes backed up, and not being able to see where they were going was unpleasant too.

During the long hours of travelling, there were a few stops, when the girls were able to unlock the van to allow her to get out and stretch her legs, but they were always mindful of being caught with a stowaway.

★   ★   ★

They were in a vast, noisy army camp and Vera was amazed to see so many army personnel milling about wearing various, mostly khaki, uniforms. And huge dumps of ammunition and petrol cans — and other stores were stacked everywhere.

'Come on,' said Susie, 'I've managed to scrounge a meal ticket for you. But slip my spare jacket on and you'll pass as a NAAFI gal.'

Vera didn't argue, she was in need of some sustenance.

In the long queue waiting for her meal, Susie and Doreen did their best to hide her in the crowd of service personnel. And because there was an air of excitement about the coming invasion, the chatter was loud, everyone was wondering about their part in the Allied landing, and glad to laugh at a joke to hide their apprehension. So Vera went unnoticed.

The girls were returning to the NAAFI van, ready to start off again, when a loud female voice assailed them.

'Salter. Thornhill. What are you up to?'

'Oh!' exclaimed Susie, 'That's our manageress.'

A square shaped older NAAFI woman shouted at them as she marched towards them.

'What are you doing with a bicycle in your van?'

Seeing Doreen and Susie struck like frightened rabbits as the manageress's piercing eyes shot at them, Vera owned up saying, 'It belongs to me.'

'Who is she?' Dulcie Swanton swung around to give Vera a look that suggested she was something the cat brought in.

But Vera was quite up to her. Fishing out her identity card Vera held it up for the manageress to see saying, 'I am a supervisor from the Ministry of Food.'

Vera had the card snatched from her and it was scrutinised. Then Vera herself was examined.

'Why are you wearing a NAAFI jacket?'

'Well, as I have to get to Selsey with a message for Colonel Parkington, and your girls kindly offered me a lift, I thought I might be useful as an extra pair of hands, serving tea, and meals.'

'What makes you think you can do our job?'

'Well, I am a Cordon Bleu chef.'

'And you are always saying you need more cooks,' added Doreen. Dulcie Swanton was dumbstruck.

'Certainly I can do with some expertise with the cooking, but we're not serving officer's lunches.'

'I feed people in the British Restaurants,' Vera told her boldly, 'so I know how to prepare good, plain meals. I've been doing it for some time.'

Now it was Miss Swanton's turn to look abashed.

'Well, I suppose you think we have a kitchen prepared when we get to the coast — we haven't.'

Vera replied, 'That's where I might be of some help to you. I can assist you to set up a canteen kitchen. I'll be a great help.'

'What about that message you have for the colonel?'

'I will, of course, have to deliver it to him as soon as possible.' Vera went on to explain her urgent need to get the military pouch to her husband.

The outcome was that Vera spent the next part of her journey to Selsey being driven in the manageress's van as a passenger. And having their catering work to discuss they soon became much more friendly.

★   ★   ★

It was dark, and raining heavily, when they arrived at their destination. Going towards the camp, Vera was staggered to see the amount of supplies piled up everywhere ready to be taken over the channel by ships and boats and on to the Mulberry dock into occupied France.

The importance of her husband's work hit her forcibly.

'I must get to the command office and see if Geoff is there,' she explained to Dulcie.

And, Miss Dulcie Swanton, who'd been much impressed by Vera's knowledge of catering, and organising kitchens, drove immediately around to the office so that Vera could make enquiries.

Eventually Vera was shown into a room full of maps and clusters of busily talking officers. A tall gangling officer came to speak to her.

'Your husband was parachuted into France last night, ma'am.'

Vera felt sick. She stood blinking at the officer, unable to think of anything to say other than, 'He needs this message.' She produced the military pouch.

'May I look at the dispatch and see if it is of importance to him?'

Vera nodded.

'You say it was delivered after he left home?'

'It was,' Vera found her voice.

The officer took the pouch and strolled over to talk to another man, who opened it and after looking at it he then replaced the document and came towards her.

'Colonel Parkington would have found this information useful. But there is no way I can get it to him now. I'm sorry you came all this way for nothing,' he said giving her a weak smile. Then he was called away, and Vera stood feeling tired and dejected.

It was clear planning was going ahead for the invasion, which seemed imminent. Everyone was busy. She picked up the pouch, which had been left on a table.

*   *   *

Dulcie Swanton's van had gone when she walked to leave the hut. Only her

34

bike was left propped up against the hut wall. But seeing the pouring rain she stayed undercover waiting for it to stop, so that she could go and find the NAAFI canteen.

But the rain continued. Relentlessly.

She leaned against the door frame for ages looking out miserably at the British summertime weather!

But she wasn't surprised to see people scuttling about in their water-proofs — and she even heard laughter and someone whistling. It was the typical British spirit to keep cheerful, and it gave her some succour to carry on with her important quest to find Geoff.

But how?

It was by chance that she overheard her husband's name mentioned by a couple of Americans dressed in combat uniforms leaving the building.

Running after them she caught them up saying, 'I'm Colonel Parkington's wife and I need to get some informa-tion to him. Urgently.'

The soldiers stopped and one turned to her saying, 'Well, ma'am. I guess he's now in France.'

Intuition made her ask, 'I know that. Are you planning to go there? I need to get this to him.' She held out the pouch for them to see.

They looked at each other.

'Yep. We're going on a raiding party. But we're not offering to carry mail for a Limey colonel.'

From somewhere deep inside her, Vera knew she must jump at the chance to go with them to France with the message. She'd no idea of what she would find when she got there — except the enemy. But someone might know where Geoff was — the underground might be able to locate him. And as the invasion would be taking place very soon she would have to hide until she could come back home.

'Please let me come with you,' she said impulsively. 'I must do my best to find my husband.'

'He won't like it if his pretty wife gets killed.'

'I'll have to take my chance, like everyone else,' Vera said boldly. 'I believe this pouch contains information about something he needs to make so that it's safe for many people going over there with stores after the invasion.'

The soldiers looked at the determination on Vera's face, and then each other.

'OK, ma'am, follow us. Our leader will decide.'

Danger Is All Around

Vera had always found most Americans had an easy-going manner, but they were also sticklers for rules. Meeting the members of the raiding party, she found unnerving.

They examined her, her identity card and the military pouch she had for Geoff with brusque thoroughness. And after she was subjected to a grilling by the leader of the raid — as if she might be an enemy spy — she felt so dazed she wasn't sure she wanted to risk her life and go with them.

Argumentative as usual, Vera looked up at them and said clearly, 'I know it is a secret. But I know nothing about the invasion plans.'

'But you know we are going to attack in Normandy.'

'So do you. And the Germans are just as likely to capture you.'

'Lady, you carry a military pouch with vitally important information.'

'The information in this pouch is in code. I don't understand it — and I doubt if it will mean anything to the Germans either. And even if they did manage to decipher it, it won't be of any help to them — it's only useful for us.'

One soldier grabbed her.

'Do you know what could happen to you if you are caught? The Gestapo are ruthless.'

Vera shuddered, but put on a brave face.

'Of course I don't know what will happen to me if, and when, I get to France.'

'Ma'am,' the leader shouted at her. 'We don't care what happens when you get over there. As long as you keep your mouth shut if you get captured. Just remember you don't know nothin' about us, or where the invasion is taking place. OK?'

Vera thought that even if she was

39

unfortunate enough to be caught by the Germans, she doubted if they would give her a harder time than these Americans.

But worse was to come. She was not prepared for the most terrifying journey of her life. The sea was in a fury and the heavens poured down incessant rain. Feeling as miserable as she'd ever felt in her life, Vera began to wish she could die before she got to the coast of France.

However, she did arrive to find herself in the early morning in Normandy. Battered, cold and lost — because the men she came with had abandoned her hours ago.

Fortunately, she had two things in her favour. One was she had taken her cranky bicycle so it would enable her to get about. The other was that she had been blessed with an excellent French teacher at school.

But where should she start looking for Geoff?

She decided to bike to the nearest

village and ask at a shop.

The mouth-watering smell of newly baked bread led her to La Boulangerie. The trouble was, she hadn't any French money. Not a sou.

She stood feeling very English, and uncertain. But what she didn't expect was that a woman came swiftly along the pavement and, without saying a word, beckoned her.

Struck that she stood out like a foreigner, Vera wondered if she'd been recognised by the Gestapo. Her breathing pounded with fright. But then she noticed the middle-aged woman looked nondescript, and that's what agents tried to be so that they didn't attract attention. Perhaps she'd been found by friends not foes?

'Come along,' the woman said as she brushed by her.

For once, Vera didn't argue, she wheeled her bicycle alongside the woman whose quick footsteps took them to a large stone house just outside the village. The old property had a wall

41

around it. They walked through the gate and into a pleasant tiled courtyard.

Vera just had time to look up at the weather-beaten house, with its peeling paint and shuttered windows when she heard footsteps.

'Vera! What in the world are you doing here?'

It was Geoff!

Her heart pounding with joy, Vera felt tears of relief seeing her tall husband dressed looking very French in a shirt with rolled up sleeves, a neckerchief and beret.

'Geoff!' she cried with delight as she ran over to greet him.

But, as she came near, she noticed he looked extremely angry.

'We received a call to say a courier was on the way, but I was not expecting you!'

He sounded so unwelcoming. Her footsteps slowed. He was not going to greet her by taking her in his arms and kissing her.

Puzzled, Vera stopped in front of him

and taking the military pouch from her skirt waistband where she'd been carrying it, she offered it to him saying, 'I brought this message which arrived soon after you left home. I thought you would need it . . . '

He almost snatched the pouch from her and opening it, strode away from her and began to read the contents as though she didn't matter.

Welling up inside her was acute disappointment. She had suffered so much to bring him the message and now he was ignoring her! In fact, he seemed to be furious with her.

Feeling someone nudging her elbow, she looked to see the woman who had bought her to the house indicating that she should come in the house.

A large cup of coffee and a freshly baked roll helped to pacify her as she sat in the French kitchen.

After a while Vera became aware that many people were coming and going and snatches of French she heard suggested the furtive nature of their activities. And when two men arrived with rifles slung over their shoulders, she guessed this house was a safe house for agents and saboteurs.

Exhausted after her travels she was pleased when she was shown a bed inside the house, and lying down was soon asleep.

★　★　★

Vera had no idea what time it was when she awoke. She ached from head to toe and was glad just to remain where she was lying down.

But she was relieved to have found Geoff — and had been able to give him the message.

However, as she lay there, she wondered how she was going to get home. Geoff didn't seem to want to acknowledge her, and the house was full of busy agents, all preparing for the invasion as they were in England.

I must just keep myself scarce. Hidden. Until the invasion is over —

which I hope and pray will be successful.

Then after a while she thought, I'd love a cup of tea — and a wash.

That desire increased until she got up and finding a bathroom, she was able to wash and change her underwear, which she had packed in her knapsack. But, seeing the ladder in her stocking, she chuckled, wishing she'd asked one of the Americans for some nylon stockings they were known to carry in their pockets.

Gingerly finding her way to the kitchen she found it empty. So filling a kettle from a jug of water she got from the pump at the sink, and taking a hunk of bread from a long French loaf on the table she was about to eat her breakfast — when she heard footsteps on the tiled floor.

Turning to see who it was opening the door she smiled as Geoff came into the kitchen with a frown on his face.

'Get me a coffee too, will you?' he said casually as though they were at home.

'Yes, sir,' she replied sharply, but he didn't seem to notice her sarcasm. He sat down on a chair and put his elbows on the table and his hands over his face.

Alarmed, Vera went over and put her hand on his shoulder.

'Are you all right?'

He shrugged off her hand saying, 'No. No. Nothing is certain. Except we are going to be bombed, heavily, very soon.'

'Oh dear!'

'You may very well say, Oh dear! Being under a bombing raid is murder. I've known it . . . you haven't. Everything gets shattered. You may not survive.'

Vera didn't like the sound of that.

'Haven't you a shelter?'

He didn't reply.

She made the coffee and brought him a cup saying, 'Wasn't that information I brought you any use?'

'Of course it was.'

Vera was pleased about that. But he didn't seem to be.

She sipped her coffee and said, 'Well

I suppose I'd better see about getting back to England.'

'Easier said than done.'

So that was the crux of the matter. Geoff was pleased to get the information she'd brought him. But he now had the problem of getting her home safely. So she realised she had added to his worries.

'Listen, Geoff,' she said looking into his eyes and longing to kiss him, 'I got here on my own, knowing it was a dangerous thing to do and I'll get back on my own. Forget about me. I'll hide somewhere, and once the invasion troops have come I'll manage to get a lift back — somehow.'

'What if the Germans throw you back into the sea?'

'Oh, they won't do that. Churchill wouldn't allow it!'

Geoff's strained face changed as he began to laugh.

'Oh Vera, you're quite a gal!'

Vera was pleased to see his pent up tension being released. He looked at her with deep affection despite shaking his head.

'Let's hope you're right,' he said, 'But I am right about the bombing.'

Longing for him to take her in his arms, she lowered her eyes. She had to be brave. Nothing would remove them both from the danger around them.

'Yes,' she said with a sigh, 'I believe you.'

Then glancing out of the window at the peaceful garden, she gave a shudder. She'd been to London and seen the results of the bombing there to know the devastation it caused — and the deaths and injuries.

'Don't think that I came to France for the fun of it. I really believed you needed the information that was in that pouch — and I couldn't think of any other way of making sure you got it.'

Suddenly he bent forward and kissed her cheek.

'Yes, it was important. It doesn't improve the chances of Mulberry being a success. But it will help my job of setting it up here. So I do thank you for bringing it. But now it is your safety that bothers me . . . I don't know what to do with you. Deception is vital — the Germans mustn't know what we are planning.

'You know enough to assist the enemy in that if they get to know about the invasion being here, they will bring down reinforcements to this area and throw us off the beaches when we try to land. You are a potential risk to the whole operation.'

Vera realised she had helped him by delivering the pouch but unwittingly she'd added to his worries too. What could she say that would make him forget her?

'Listen,' she said, 'I am one person. You have hundreds to think about. Get on with your job as if I am not here. I know you have a lot to do. Please try and forget I am here. I promise you I will lie low.'

He stood up and went to the window looking out at the sky as if he expected it to be filled with aircraft dropping parachutes — or seeing heavy bombers droning overhead.

'Yes, I still have a lot to do. I must go now. The invasion may take place any day.'

She stood too and went over to him, slipping her arm around his waist until he turned and held her tight.

'Promise to look after yourself,' he said in a cracked voice, and kissing her forehead before releasing her he strode out of the house.

Feeling devastated she heard his footsteps fade away.

She went back and sat down at the table. Alone, and for the first time feeling certain she might never see him again. The fear of being killed or injured or captured by the Gestapo — thoughts such as these raced through her mind.

What would the future bring for them both?

And the other people using the safehouse?

Cruel Words Are Spoken

After the shock of knowing the dangers that lurked around her, Vera realised her next problem was where to hide. Unlike the British who had built underground shelters, the French in the area were not expecting to be attacked and the house only had a wine cellar.

But did she fancy waiting in a damp cellar for hours, perhaps days, for danger to come? She daren't go far away from the house, no farther than the walled garden anyway.

It was not only her safety she had to think of. It was all the people using the house who might be shot, or captured, if she was caught.

So her next concern was boredom. Sitting waiting to be bombed, or raided by the Germans, was a dreadful feeling as the long hours dragged by. Everyone who came to the house seemed to be busy and Vera longed to have something useful to do. She was used to working, not sitting about being idle.

Should she offer to clean the house or wash their clothes — or even feed the hens that were clucking around the garden?

Of course, she smiled. She could cook a meal for them! She was a well-qualified Cordon Bleu chef — well used to French cooking. And her war service was cooking hundreds of meals using stringent wartime food rations — so she was also well able to make do with what was available.

It lightened her mood to have something positive — and useful to do. The men and women risking their lives to liberate France needed good sustenance to keep them healthy and able to do their work. And all they seemed to have was endless cups of coffee and bread someone fetched from the bakery once or twice a day.

Standing in the beautiful country garden, aware of the sweet smells of nature, Vera's mind raced.

A chicken dish would be easy to make if she had the ingredients and the wood fire kitchen range lit to put the cooking pot on. Then here in the large garden there was bound to be a vegetable patch with a few onions and carrots, herbs — and knowing the French they would have a bottle of wine tucked away somewhere.

Yes, it is possible, she mused. 'But where am I going to get some butter from?' she said aloud to a cat who sat on the wall cleaning its paws. 'The French use a lot of butter in their cooking.'

'This is a country area, with dairy farms around, I dare say I can get some for you.'

It was Geoff, back from wherever he'd been.

Vera gulped back her emotion at seeing him again. It brought tears to her eyes just knowing he was still alive.

She said, 'I thought it would be a good idea to cook a meal for everyone.'

'Excellent.'

'Can you get some wood for me? I'll need to get the range going.'

★   ★   ★

Vera was soon in her element, occupied finding some onions, parsley, thyme and bay leaves from the garden. Soon she was washing the vegetables and plucking the chickens while Geoff went off to find some butter.

She felt happy preparing the meal, and received many delighted smiles from the people coming and going from the house.

'Haven't you got any work to do?' she asked Geoff when he'd come back with a bundle of firewood and a big pat of butter.

'Nope. Not now. My work is at a standstill until the invasion is over. Then, if our troops manage to get a foothold on French soil and drive the enemy from the coast, I'll have to help get the Mulberry B dock in place.'

With delight Vera realised she'd have

Geoff's company for a few days. They had drifted apart since their wedding and with the stress of their wartime work. But now they were together with plenty of time, and able to renew their close relationship — although in a situation that they least expected their love affair to continue and thrive.

The old tiled French country kitchen had old-fashioned cooking utensils — but all she needed.

Geoff teased her saying, 'When I first recruited you to cook meals in the town hall kitchen in Lynn, you said you wouldn't even scrub a carrot in it!'

Vera, who was chopping onions rapidly as a professional chef with a sharpened knife, laughed.

'Yes, I remember I was rather spoilt after working in a first class restaurant. It was a shock having to cook cheap meals helped only by untrained assistants.'

'But I knew you were sterling and would manage, Vera.'

Flattered, Vera smiled and replied,

'Just as the British engineers trust you with your work on Mulberry, Geoff.'

A shadow passed over his face and she knew he was still worried about his responsibility with setting up the floating dock.

'I wish you didn't know about it,' he muttered, squatting down and feeding the stove with small logs of wood that crackled in the fire.

'Why? It allows me to understand the heavy load of responsibility you carry. I know you are suffering from thinking of your past, and that another error may occur again. Which doesn't help you feel you can do the job, but I know you have worked so hard to get it right and you have the necessary knowledge and skills. No-one can expect more from you than that. But everyone learns from their mistakes — and you will have to. You have experience on your side.'

He didn't reply, but he went over to where she was sizzling some chopped onions in a frying pan, and took her in his arms.

'The only success I want is with you,' he said softly in her ear. 'And I'm sorry I've been so snappy over the past months.'

'Oh, Geoff, just remember, I love you. We'll get over this war together, with all its horrors and difficulties.'

He kissed her.

'Aye, aye,' shouted a man who'd come into the kitchen, 'You can't do that here! Get on with the cooking — I'm starved and those fried onions smell delicious.'

Grinning at each other Vera and Geoff parted.

Vera said, 'Why don't you put some tables and chairs out in the courtyard then there'll be plenty of room for everyone to sit down and enjoy their meal in the fresh air.'

★   ★   ★

It was a merry party of men and women, as well as some children that appeared, and who sat around the long table as Vera served the portions of chicken casserole to the hungry people.

That was her usual job — to feed the hungry with nutritious meals. And very satisfying it was for her too, to see them all tucking in. They appreciated her effort to make the meal tasty, and she had even thought to make a bowl of stewed apple with some small biscuits to go with it too as a dessert.

At the end of the meal, Vera received many compliments.

'You're a wonderful cook, Mrs Parkington.'

'That was the best meal I've ever had.'

'Geoff's a lucky man to have you as a wife.'

And the French children came up to her to say solemnly, '*Merci, Madame,*' and kissed her rosy cheek.

'Whew,' exclaimed Vera, who'd also benefited from the meal, because she hadn't had one for some time. 'I'm glad they all liked the food. Now for the washing up, Geoff.' Because just as the diners had come from nowhere — they had melted away.

Piles of dirty plates, bowls, knives and forks and empty wine glasses needed to be washed and put away.

'You ought to feel proud of yourself,' remarked Geoff, giving her a hand with the chore, 'you cooked the meal superbly well.'

'Thank you,' Vera replied as she washed a pan, 'I feel pleased you think my journey here has been worthwhile.'

'I didn't say that. I wish you hadn't come. It is far too dangerous here, and you being here is a constant worry for me.'

Vera flared up.

'I'm a worry to you! What do you think you are for me? I worry all the time about what you are doing — '

'I have no choice. I'm in the army and I am doing my duty. You are not. You need not have come.'

Vera turned to shout at him, 'How would you have got that information you needed if I hadn't come, eh?'

'I would have managed I expect.'

Vera was now upset and furious with him.

'Well, that's a fine thing to say. You could have managed without the message I brought you. I dare say you could manage without me too. Well then, go and get yourself killed — I don't care!'

He threw down the tea towel he was holding and stamped out of the kitchen.

Vera stood horrified.

What had she said to him in anger?

It wasn't true — just the opposite, she did care. She cared very much what happened to him.

Tidying away the kitchen things, she felt even more remorseful. Whatever had got into her?

★ ★ ★

The burden of guilt lay on her for days because he avoided her. She didn't see him at all. Over and over again she thought about her temper tantrum and why it had happened. She had hours alone to think about it — which was dreadful.

Of course she was under stress, trying to make the best of a dangerous situation she was in. Hoping to find a way to get back to England, but realising she had to lay low and not be captured.

She thought of writing a note for Geoff, but would it ever get to him? He seemed to have vanished.

But she had said she didn't want him.

The only way she could cope with her distress, and feel that her presence there was of use, was to continue to cook a midday meal for everyone who came for it. And a good many people turned up.

Some brought food — a little meat, or flour or olives and vegetables, whatever they had, and Vera was adept at making the best of what she was given and preparing a tasty dish for them all. They all seemed to enjoy what she cooked. And they praised her.

Normally she would have felt elated, but as Geoff wasn't there she felt distraught. He needed a good meal and he was avoiding not only eating with them all — he was avoiding her.

She was being well punished for her sharp, careless words to him.

★ ★ ★

It was all too quiet around the house. But one night she heard sounds like bombing in the far distance. She huddled under the bedclothes, but knew if a bomb landed on the house she would probably not survive — or she might be badly injured.

Next day she worked hard to prepare an oxtail casserole. It was ready for everyone, but few people came. All the agents were missing. It was such a shame that in the summer weather she had no fridge to store the dish until they turned up.

The long dining table, which was usually busy with hungry people coming and going, was almost empty.

'Where is everyone?' she asked a young mother with two small children.

The woman shrugged. 'I don't know.'

Several old men were there. They enjoyed their meal and thanked her before they shuffled away to play boules.

Worried, Vera ate hardly anything herself, and began to clear the dishes away when she heard the sound of people outside.

'Ah, here they are at last!' she said, thinking she might have to warm up the meal, but when the courtyard gates opened, Vera's mouth dropped open in horror.

In marched a small troop of German soldiers carrying rifles.

Vera clutched the oven cloth she had in her hands as she watched the enemy soldiers crowd into the courtyard and began to search around — shouting to each other in their guttural language, and even entering the house without asking anyone if they may.

Finding she was taking deep breaths and unable to move, Vera's brain whirled to think what she should do.

Get on with what you were doing. Pretend you are busy. They will soon go away.

Vera Has A Secret

As Vera tried to control her fear and began to busy herself in the kitchen, doing the ordinary kitchen jobs, she didn't hear the German soldiers and thought they had gone.

Thank goodness for that!

Then, aware that someone was staring at her, she swung around to see a helmeted face looking at her through the window.

Horrified, she almost dropped the pan she was carrying.

They haven't gone!

She was desperately trying to think what she should do when the man began tapping at the window, seeking her attention.

All she could think of was to try to pretend to be a French housewife, because she could understand and speak French, and would not be

expected to understand German —
which was just as well.

Going to the window, Vera was struck
by the soldier's penetrating blue eyes.
They seemed to see right through her.
Terrified, she began to sweat.

But he couldn't possibly know she
was an Englishwoman, could he?

The window was open and as the
soldier took off his helmet she saw he
was a young man with flaxen hair. He
pointed to his mouth.

What on earth could he want?

He said something in German.

'*Das Essen*,' said another soldier who
had joined him.

Vera suddenly understood. The soldiers wanted some food.

Well, she had the casserole she'd
prepared for the agents, who hadn't
turned up for their meal — so why not
offer it to the Germans? It was better
than wasting the food. And it wouldn't
mean she was going to give away any
military secrets.

With hammering heartbeats, Vera

went to open the kitchen door and indicated that the six soldiers should come in, and be seated at the kitchen table.

'*Guten Morgen!*' they chorused as they entered and removed their helmets.

The rabbit stew really needed to be heated, but she downright refused to heat it up for the enemy troops. They would have it as it was and like it.

After doling out soup plates full of the casserole she watched while they devoured the food as if they were starving. Perhaps they were? The German army was known to be an efficient fighting unit, but ruthless. And clearing away the cooking pot — hoping not to drop it and show how nervous she felt — she watched them surreptitiously and noticed how young some of the soldiers were.

Little more than sixteen years old she guessed. And they probably missed home cooking, and their civilian life. They had been rounded up to fight in

Hitler's army like sheep to the slaughterhouse.

She could find nothing objectionable about the four young men's manners as they thanked her when every scrap of food had gone.

But Vera was not so pleased when as they left they wanted to kiss her! But she reasoned that would be considered polite in Germany to thank their hostess for a good meal. So she tried not to stiffen and show that they were on opposite sides.

One lingered, clearly wanting to continue to talk to her, and Vera began to realise the young man wanted to see her again. So she showed him her wedding ring, and he bowed, clicked his heels together and walked away with the others — who all turned and waved to her.

She felt quite shaky when they had gone.

She'd been lucky. They were not the worst type of German soldiers.

Something caught her eye in the

bushes and she gasped when Geoff stepped out, with a revolver in his hand.

'Thank your lucky stars, they've gone,' he said putting his gun back into its holster.

She ran to him automatically. 'Geoff! Oh Geoff — I was so scared . . . '

'So was I, Vera. I was ready to shoot them.'

'They,' she sobbed, 'were all right. Just lads like our lads.'

'Only on the wrong side.'

Vera took the large handkerchief Geoff offered her and wiped her eyes. 'Yes,' she said.

Geoff released her and looked at her with much affection, but said firmly, 'It's not over — it has only just begun.'

Tears welled in her eyes as she clung to him, and he comforted her, rubbing her back as he held her close.

'You're too late for dinner,' Vera retorted, 'they ate it all.'

'I don't care what they ate — as long as you're safe, Vera.'

She chuckled, partly from relief that

the danger had passed and that Geoff looked fit and well — although she was sure he'd more frown lines on his brow since she saw him last.

Suddenly aware there were other people in the courtyard, she said with surprise, 'The others have come back and I suppose they want a meal — and the Germans have eaten it all.'

Geoff smiled at her ruefully.

'I'm sure a good cook like you can rustle something up for us.'

Vera gulped. She hadn't quite got over the frightening experience of feeling helpless in the presence of enemy soldiers — although she now realised the agents were probably hiding and keeping an eye on her all the time.

She stepped away from Geoff, and looked around at the brave men and women who were prepared to risk their lives to free Europe from Hitler's grip and said, 'I daresay I can.'

'Don't take long about it,' said Geoff, becoming like a commanding officer again, 'The invasion is due in twenty-four hours and it may be the last proper meal we'll have for days.'

Vera froze. What on earth could she give them to eat?

Then her training kicked in. Eggs. Omelettes. Salad with cheese, and some fresh fruit. She could manage that very quickly and easily. She'd collected some eggs only this morning and picked some soft-skinned pink apricots from the tree in the garden which were deliciously ripe and ready to eat.

'I'll give you a hand,' Geoff offered, and with his towering strength by her side Vera was soon more concerned with eking out the small amount of butter she had left to fry the omelettes than thinking about anything that had frightened her earlier.

Someone, bless them, had nipped out and brought in some long French sticks of fresh bread, and soon the agents were enjoying a meal as they usually did.

But it was not a usual occasion, as

Vera soon found out.

'This is the last meal we will have together,' announced Geoff standing up with his wine glass in his hand. 'We are all on alert now for action.'

Everyone's eyes turned towards the tall Englishman who perhaps had one of the most difficult and responsible tasks in the whole D-Day operation.

He continued, 'We all come from different homes. Some of us are French and are fighting for France to be liberated. Some of us are British, and we are going to fight to put the Germans back where they belong — in Germany. And I know several of you are from other countries the Germans have overrun. But we all hope that our efforts, however small, and perhaps our lives will be given . . . for the cause of Peace in Europe, for those dear to us at home, and our children.'

After this solemn speech everyone was silent for a while, deep in their own thoughts of why they were there, and doubtless thinking about what could happen to them in the next few days.

But the quiet period of reflection did not remain for long. After they had all held up their glasses and drunk their wine, a spontaneous party started with singing, shouting and even dancing.

Vera, being typically British, felt shy and looked with amazement at their jollity. But soon she was laughing at the antics and she felt her hand taken and she was pulled into the dancing circle, and she found their enthusiasm infectious and was soon capering about like everyone else.

Exhausted after their exertions, everyone sat down again and as their goodbyes with kisses and hugs took place, one agent called out, 'Vera!'

Alarmed, Vera found everyone looking at her.

A voice called out, 'A toast to the pretty lady who has fed us so well!'

Cries of approval, whistles, and banging on the table showed that they all endorsed that statement.

'Stand up and say something,' said

Geoff, giving her a prod.

Red-faced, Vera felt tongue-tied.

'I don't know what to say,' she whispered in all honesty. 'All I've done is to provide a few meals. These brave people are going off to fight . . . '

'Napoleon said an army fights on its stomach,' chuckled Geoff.

That was a well-known saying. She was sure they had all learned that at school. But, as a nutritionist she knew that good food was essential to everybody, and she was delighted to know that she had helped in her small way to assist these fighters for freedom.

But what could she say on this poignant occasion? Everyone was looking at her. She must think of something significant to say.

Suddenly the words of a song came into her mind. Vera Lynn used to sing it and she liked Vera Lynn. Standing she began singing the popular song, *We'll Meet Again*.

To her relief she heard the English people among them recognise the song and begin to sing with her.

It made a fitting ending to the memorable meal, and soon the courtyard became empty as everyone drifted off to do their allotted tasks.

Still breathing heavily with the exertion of singing and dancing Vera was taken aside by Geoff who held her close and whispered, 'I meant it when I said the invasion is on its way. You must hide until you see British soldiers around and know they have taken this part of Normandy.

'Now you can't stay here any longer. I have marked on this little map an underground shelter where you can hide with other local people. It may take several days before you can come out and you will hear the noise of battle around you. But keep your head down, and pray we are successful. Now, promise me you will go there, Vera.'

Looking up into his eyes, she could tell he was as worried about her safety as he was about his role in establishing the floating dock.

'Of course, I'll go there, Geoff. You mustn't worry about me. God alone knows if I will survive . . . '

She didn't think it was the right moment to tell him that it was not only her survival that was at stake — she felt sure she was going to have his child.

The tears in his eyes showed her that he didn't want to part from her, that he was fully aware of the horrors of war that would descend on them very soon. And for one awful moment her courage left her and all she could do was to cling to him — she didn't want to part from him or let any harm come to him either.

But just as the agents had gone off to fight courageously, not knowing their fate — so must they.

'Geoffrey Parkington, I love you more than I can say,' she said sniffing and wiping her eyes, 'but like everyone else we must get on and do our duty. I'll keep you in my heart whatever happens, and please God, you will be safe, and come home . . . ' she was going to say, 'to us,' but she didn't like to add to his worries and responsibilities, by saying he might be a father by then, so she just said, 'very soon.'

'I sincerely hope so. But you know the conflict won't be over for some time . . . now you must leave this place before it gets dark and find the shelter. Keep safe for me. Goodbye, my love,' he croaked.

He kissed her forehead and lips and without another word he gave her the little map, then swung around and marched off without turning back.

★   ★   ★

She was glad she'd been left with all the washing up. It gave her something to do putting away all the kitchen pans and crockery. She'd become fond of the house and garden that had provided her with somewhere pleasant to live during the summer days she'd been there. She wanted to leave it in order. Some French family had allowed the agents to

77

use the house, but after the war they would want their home back — if it survived.

She loved the courtyard and the chickens that roamed wild with the other wildlife that lived there. The wild grasses and flowers — the sheer beauty and smells of nature she'd enjoyed.

And she regretted not being able to feed the old men and the mother with her young children any more. She couldn't even say goodbye to them, and wish them well.

But Geoff was right. She shouldn't stay there in case the soldiers came back, and not all the German soldiers were as pleasant as the ones she'd fed. So she needed to leave and shelter from the coming bombing raids.

Practically minded as ever, Vera collected her clean washing from a bush where she'd put it to dry that morning, and regretted the ladder she still had in her stocking, thinking that if she met some Americans she'd ask them for some nylon stockings.

She packed her knapsack with what she considered might come in useful. It was like Geoff's car, which always contained things people found useful like Aladdin's cave.

Her bag, on a smaller scale, was stuffed with everything that might come in handy. She even put in some bread she'd dried out in the dying oven heat to make rusks.

Then, with a last look at the old French house she'd enjoyed living in, she found her old bicycle and set off, with cranking pedals to the shelter Geoff had told her to find.

It was an eerie feeling for Vera to think that a huge invasion force was about to shatter the peace of the beautiful countryside around her as she pedalled along the country road.

It was shocking, awful, horrifying to think that it was going to happen. But she knew it would. And there was nothing she could do to prevent it happening. The result of it might be that she was killed, or wounded. The same applied to all the people involved in D-Day and Overlord — the names given to the battles ahead. But Vera was determined to do what she could do. And the first was to protect herself and her unborn child from danger.

She was so deep in her thoughts that she almost wobbled off her bicycle as she saw a military vehicle ahead. It was blocking the road.

A Narrow Escape

German soldiers were strolling about, lolling against their vehicle and smoking, as though they were waiting for something.

Vera gripped her bicycle handlebars tightly. What should she do? They must have seen her coming. If she turned around and pedalled off they might think she was trying to avoid them and come after her.

During her first days in France an agent had given her false identity papers that all French people had to carry with them and she now knew why they had impressed on her that she must have them.

Her chief worry as she cycled closer to the soldiers was that she knew a secret she must not divulge — the time and place of the invasion. Even a few hours of the enemy knowing that might make all the difference to the Allies successful landings on the Normandy beaches.

The heavy burden of knowing that, as so many top planners, generals and agents did, suddenly felt as if it was placed on her shoulders. Vera felt as if she could hardly breathe.

But she must carry on as though she was only biking to the next village to see her grandmother.

The soldiers were hanging around, looking bored as often soldiers were when they had no work to do. But they paid attention to the pretty young woman cycling towards them — pleased to see she might provide them with some entertainment.

'Halt!'

A young soldier made a great show of stopping her, making the other soldiers laugh at his remarks — which were in German, so Vera couldn't understand what he said. Which, she felt, was probably just as well.

The soldiers didn't appear too

threatening either, and Vera felt able to breathe properly again.

Vera almost laughed as she put on her brakes, which were a bit worn, and she skidded towards a soldier who just hopped out of the way before she crashed into him.

The other soldiers began to laugh and make raucous comments about her driving, so Vera had to apologise, in French, she remembered just in time.

'Fraulein, your papers please.'

Vera knew where they were — with the map Geoff had given her in her pocket and she wished she'd had the sense to separate the two. But she had the wit to begin to search for the papers as if she didn't know where she'd put them.

The soldier stood patiently while she chatted to him in French about visiting her old grandmother who needed some provisions, and she intended to cook the old lady a meal.

By distracting the soldier's attention, she was able to take out the identity papers and leave the map in her pocket.

With a shaking hand she offered the identity papers to the soldier and hoped the agents had done a good job making them look authentic.

Holding her breath, Vera looked down at her front tyre and noticed she had a puncture.

The soldier recognised the French identity papers and to her relief, only gave them a cursory glance, and gave them back to her.

The soldier had followed her eyes and noticed the flat tyre too.

Vera could hardly believe what happened next. The soldier took her bike from her and began to look for the puncture.

Remembering she had a puncture kit — a small, oblong tin box — in her bicycle bag, Vera looked for it. Then she handed it to the soldier who, opening it, took out a small tube of glue, and a rubber patch. Then he set about mending her puncture!

Well, blow me down! I gave some

Germans a meal — and now one is mending my bicycle tyre. Tit for tat. One good turn deserves another!

When he'd finished an expert job mending the tyre, he noticed the creaking pedals, and went off, coming back with a can of oil. And soon her screechy pedals were well-oiled and working smoothly. Last of all he looked at her brake pads and adjusted them so that they worked properly.

German efficiency!

Vera was flabbergasted.

The repairs were complete and Vera was thanking the soldier, when a bellowed order was heard. Every soldier came to attention. Then as the soldiers rushed to line up by the side of the road, and moved their vehicle off the centre of the road, Vera felt alarmed.

What was happening?

It was clear to her that they were waiting for someone to come along the road.

Was it a high-ranking German officer coming to review the coastal defences?

But Vera had the sense not to wait to find out. Getting on her bicycle, she rode off as fast as she could — and she found she just whisked along the road, with a plump front tyre, and easy-to-turn pedals.

What a narrow escape she'd had from the enemy.

★   ★   ★

It was only a little time after that she heard the sound of a car coming behind her.

Before she had time to consider what to do it had raced by her at such speed she fell off her bike. But she had time to glimpse the grim face of a capped German officer in the back of the car.

Was it the famous German, Rommel, who had been beaten by Montgomery in Africa?

It could have been.

As she picked herself up and noticed yet another run in her stockings, she wished she was at home and could mend them as she usually did with her sewing mushroom and needle and thread. Make and mend. And the Germans she'd found out were pretty good at that too.

But home was another world. Right now she was lost, somewhere near the Normandy coast in France, with a huge invasion force about to descend on the area.

She felt herself shivering as she consulted her map and mounted her bicycle again. Would she ever find this shelter Geoff had told her to go to?

What she wanted more than anything was a cup of tea!

★ ★ ★

It seemed hours later when she approached a village that she recognised the row of trees Geoff had drawn for her on the map. Somewhere around must be the shelter.

She was cautious, approaching the quiet village with stealth. She'd learned enough by now to know she had to be careful. She hadn't met any nasty Germans yet, but she knew she'd been fortunate not to. Getting off her bicycle she wheeled it slowly towards the houses, looking around to see if she could spot anyone.

She supposed it was not unusual for people to be having their evening meal at this late hour and that was why there was no-one about. But it didn't comfort her. The whole place seemed too empty. Where was everyone? Hiding in their cellars because the word had got around that they were vulnerable as the Allies were coming?

Vera walked through the deserted street, and began to think she would have to knock on a door, when she was taken unawares, hearing aircraft over-head. Before she could consider what to do she realised the place was under attack.

The tremendous roar of the low-flying planes frightened her and she automatically crouched down. Seconds later the tremendous earth-shaking sounds of bombs exploding made her cower near a doorway.

Shaken, she remained there for a while until she began to realise this was only a taste of what was to come and she must find the shelter.

With hands that would not keep still, she took out the little map she'd been given. Making herself look at it although her eyes made the directions swim in front of her, she saw it suggested the shelter was the other side of the village.

Get going! You can't stay here unprotected.

But she felt so scared she just didn't want to move. Then she remembered Geoff, and her unborn child. She had to save herself from danger for their sake.

Everyone was frightened in wartime. Every soldier, sailor, as well as those under attack. What was the song she knew so well?

Pack up your troubles in your old kit bag and smile, smile, smile . . .

She had got herself into this mess, no-one had ordered her to go to France. Geoff was furious that she had. So she must make the best of it.

With legs that didn't want to support her, Vera picked herself, and her bicycle up, and began to make herself work out where the shelter was. Geoff's instructions had been fairly straightforward so far, so she must remain calm and figure out where the shelter was.

It was a shock seeing a bomb had landed on some houses. The dust covered everything. Shattered glass and smashed walls she had to walk over.

Only the shells of some old houses that had stood for years remained. The rest had crumbled away, revealing the private lives of people who had lived there.

She could see the colour of their bedroom wallpaper, a crooked picture still hanging on a wall. Some furniture was incredibly still in place, although most of the upper floors were gaping open.

This was the result of war. It was heartbreakingly sad.

Stumbling on she passed through the village and faced the open countryside and felt she could breathe freely again.

Ah, there was the sign she was looking for: a very small wayside chapel containing a statue, where someone had placed some flowers.

It was hearing children's voices that alerted her to the entrance of the huge underground foxhole.

Still feeling wobbly, Vera made her way down a bank to find a hundred pairs of eyes staring at her.

She didn't expect that this was going to be her hiding place for the next few days.

★   ★   ★

Speaking French helped her to make herself accepted amongst the villagers. And being with them was better than being alone. Vera soon found her time taken up with helping to amuse the children, and comfort them as the bombardment took place overhead.

There was feeding everyone to think about too. And here, Vera made herself useful, helping the village women to share what food they had brought with them into the shelter so that no-one was left to starve.

For the first time in her life Vera had periods of feeling really hungry. But knowing she was expecting a child she had to have her share of any of the food available to keep healthy.

Vera remembered later, the long hours and days she huddled with the hundred or so villagers in the shelter being a nightmare. Aware of hearing thunderous noises over them, they knew tragedies were taking place. Even the children stopped playing and became frightened — like the adults — wondering what was to become of them.

★   ★   ★

92

After days of hearing bombing, the quietness that followed was just as scary. Everyone began to talk, wondering what had happened above ground.

Jeanette, a young woman who Vera was helping with distributing the food, was concerned about some of her livestock.

'I must go and feed my goats,' she said.

Vera looked at her with apprehension. 'It may not be safe . . . '

Jeanette stared back at her.

'I've been looking out and haven't seen any sign of any soldiers about.'

Vera could understand her dilemma.

Anxious to stretch her legs and get some fresh air, Vera said impulsively, 'I'll go with you.'

Jeanette smiled saying, 'I admit I am scared of going alone, although it isn't far to the farm.'

So the two women scrambled out from underground, and cautiously viewed the surrounding countryside. It all appeared to be as normal at first. No noise, and no-one in sight.

Following Jeanette, Vera walked along the lane towards the farm. Alert, in case they had to dive under a hedge. They found nothing untoward — at first.

Suddenly Jeanette gave a cry and pointed towards a field. The gate had been smashed by a tank which had churned up the grass into muddy tracks.

Vera gasped seeing the dead cattle and grasped Jeanette's hand.

But they continued towards the farm, which seemed intact.

Jeanette murmured a prayer under her breath.

★   ★   ★

When they arrived at the goat pen the goats were alive. Jeanette filled a bucket with water and hurriedly placed it for them to drink and then another with feed and threw it into the pen.

A loud explosion made the women fall to the ground.

There had been a bomb in the goat

pen and the bucket had hit it and exploded.

Shaken by their narrow escape from death, Jeanette and Vera hugged each other, then agreed they must take great care wherever they went.

The farmhouse was unharmed, and Jeanette was able to collect a few items she wanted to take back to the shelter, while Vera wandered outside and looked towards the village.

It took her a few minutes to realise that the buildings ahead had not escaped bombardment. The spire on the church was missing. Some houses had been hit. Some people in the shelter were going to find their homes, and possessions and livestock had not survived the fighting.

And indeed, so far she had been lucky.

But what about Geoff?

Before they returned, they gathered some fruit from the orchard, and found a few eggs, then hurried back into the shelter.

How much longer would they be stuck underground?

A Dangerous Journey

Next morning uniformed men came towards the shelter and there was a hush. Everyone was afraid of what they might do to them. But Vera smiled, recognising a British officer.

It was Geoff!

Dressed in his English colonel's uniform, she rushed to put her arms around him, knowing that the Allied landings had been successful. He wouldn't be walking about in his uniform if the Germans still held the area.

'I had to come and check on you,' he said hugging her close.

'I'm all right.'

'Is there anything you need?'

She shook her head. Being with him was all she wanted.

'And your job?' she asked.

'Mulberry B for the British landings

is in place, but we'd only just got the supplies unloaded from the ships when a terrible storm blew up in the Channel, almost wrecked it. In fact, the lashing waves did wreak Mulberry A, the American floating harbour.'

Vera looked up into his eyes and expected him to cry with anguish that his long hard slog to get the harbours made and in position had failed because of the foul weather.

But he smiled. 'We waited until the storm was over, and then managed to repair Mulberry B, using part of Mulberry A that had been saved.'

'What about the American supplies?'

'The Americans managed to capture the port of Cherbourg and can use that to bring their supplies on shore.'

'So your floating dock is successful?' Vera asked the question, although she knew by the relief on his face that it was.

'Yes, it is.'

'Your worries are over.'

'No, Vera. My worry now is to get

you safely back home,' he said.

Vera had learned not to be so sure of what might happen to her — both good fortune and bad might occur. And knowing she'd had several lucky escapes from danger of various kinds already, she was now wise enough not to repeat, as she had done before, that she had got to France on her own and she could get back just as easily.

'Aren't you going back, now your job is done?'

He shook his head.

'No, it isn't. I might be in France for some time, at least until the British are able to use French ports. And German opposition is formidable. There is bitter fighting everywhere. We have still to secure all the land and make sure we are not pushed back into the sea.'

Their conversation was interrupted. People were anxious to ask when they could return to their homes.

'Be sure to tell them to take great care wherever they go,' said Vera, 'and warn them about the devastation they may see.'

Colonel Parkington's French was not as good as Vera's, but between them they were able to tell the villagers that the battle had moved from the immediate countryside and was unlikely to return. That raised a cheer. However, being told about the horrors they might find ahead of them was not easy to explain. Vera thought Geoff put it as well as anyone could.

★   ★   ★

After everyone had had the opportunity to ask questions, which Geoff and the other soldiers with him answered as best they could, the villagers collected their belongings and left.

Geoff took Vera aside.

'Your home is a long way off,' he said. 'I want you to have this pass to get back on any transport that will take you.' He handed her some papers. 'But, of course, I need not tell you that the whole coastal area is still covered with mines and obstacles. It'll be cleared in time, but you need to know where not to tread. And there may still be pockets of Germans hiding in the countryside, or German agents about ready to shoot anyone in sight.

'You won't be able to avoid coming across seeing so many dead and injured. Germans, as well as allied soldiers have been killed.

'So much carnage is hard to bear and awful to see. The army and the local people will clear it all up in time, but the pressing need is for the armies that have landed to move forward and drive the Germans back.'

Vera steeled herself to accept seeing the ravages of war. She had to go through it to reach England. Her place was at home now — to have her baby.

Should she tell him the good news?

No, once again she decided it was better she should not let him worry about her anymore than he did already. And he did appear to have aged — to have more creases on his brow.

He seemed to have become almost detached from any emotion. For some reason she thought he was like a wound up toy soldier just marching about.

Their parting was as painful as most lovers who had to part during the war. It took all Vera's inner strength to remain cheerful and wish him well, and not burst into tears at the thought of any harm that might come to him.

But as he set off in his jeep, Vera made the effort to smile and not show him how frightened she felt — for his as well as her survival — and she waved. She knew she was now physically weakened after weeks of living on any food she could get hold of. And being a nutritionist, she longed to get home as quickly as possible and prepare her body with some wholesome food for the birth of her baby.

The French families had the sadness of seeing the aftermath of the bombardment and havoc caused by the fighting that had taken place around their village.

The devastation for some was heartbreaking. But everyone helped each other to try and overcome the trauma the war had inflicted on them. As many in France rejoiced that the invasion had been a success and the Germans driven off, others mourned their dead and began to rebuild.

Jeanette's family offered Vera the chance to stay with them for a few days so that she could recover from being entombed. She was able to have a bath and wash her clothes. The job of bringing the farm back to normal began. Lost livestock had to be replaced, and mending what had been broken.

'It is so sad,' Jeanette said, 'before the Allies came the Germans left us alone to continue our lives in peace. Now look at the mess.'

Vera could sympathise with her. So many people's lives had been destroyed by Hitler's ambitions. And even now thousands of others faced catastrophe.

But all Vera could do, was what most people had to do, get on with what they were faced with. She helped Jeanette clear up the farmhouse and farmyard, and assisted her to cook a meal using what was available. Rabbit stews, pigeon pies and using herbs, fruits and vegetables from the farm.

Cooking was soothing for Vera. Several women came and helped her prepare the vegetables. Although Vera had the constant difficulty of thinking of dishes that had ingredients she had available. But she managed.

Her meals were appreciated by everyone who came to the farm hoping for food. Especially grateful were those villagers who had been bombed out of their homes and had no cooking facilities.

★   ★   ★

At last the day came when Vera was feeling stronger and felt able to travel, she said goodbye to her French friends, collected her bicycle, and set off for the coast.

The loss of having friends around her was chilling. And as she pedalled carefully, the thought of what she might see before she got home made her heart quaver — but she gritted her teeth and tried not to dwell on anything she saw.

Men digging graves, and others stacking supplies into piles just as they had been in England before she left.

Arriving at the wide expanse of beach she was immediately struck by the debris of a battle.

'Where do you think you are going, Miss?'

The bellowed question made Vera start, and turn to see a British military policeman striding towards her.

'I'm going back to England, I hope,' she shouted back.

'Well you won't get there that way. There're mines ahead. Come over here.'

It was comforting to find a British soldier.

Once she had been joined by the tough-looking man — with a revolver that was easy for him to get at — he looked her up and down suspiciously.

'Are you hoping to swim the channel, eh?'

She took out the papers Geoff had given her, and snatching them he looked them over.

Then pointing to a pillbox he barked at her, 'Go over to there. Stay with the casualties waiting to be evacuated.'

'Yes, sir,' Vera said cheekily. It was strangely reassuring being bossed around and told what to do.

It wasn't easy to push her bicycle over the churned up sand, but she didn't want to leave it in France if she could possibly take it back to England. Especially as the German soldier had repaired it for her it was like new.

But she soon forgot about it when she reached the canvas protecting the scores of injured soldiers waiting for a boat to take them home.

Almost at once she realised she could

help the nurses with tending the sick. Just being there and talking to them, or helping a Queen Alexandra's Royal Army Nurse assist an injured soldier made her useful.

★   ★   ★

The skilled nurses were amongst the first British servicewomen to come to Normandy after D-Day, but they were tired and glad of Vera's help.

Grey-faced, some of the men were shivering from pain even under their blankets and needed someone to reassure them.

A little yelp made her look to see a prone man hiding an Alsatian puppy under his blanket, which he told Vera he'd found wandering about lost.

'Don't tell the Sister I have her under my blanket,' he whispered, 'Or she'll make me give her up.'

The lad was badly wounded and she hadn't the heart to take the little animal from him.

She even managed to find a drink for the puppy when the nurses weren't looking.

Full of sympathy, she stayed and talked to him when she could.

'What's your name?'

'Fred.'

'Where do you come from?'

'Newcastle.'

Vera only had a vague idea about the North of England, but she listened to him tell about his football team and how he did the pools every week if he could afford it on his meagre soldier's pay. She held his hand and tried to comfort him as she thought his mother, or sister, or girlfriend would do.

But hours later after Vera and the soldier had been put on board a boat to be taken back to England, she found the soldier had died.

Now she had a puppy, as well as a bicycle, to take home.

'She's Expecting A Baby'

No-one took much notice of her when they landed. All the attention was given to taking the injured off the boat and into waiting ambulances. Vera hid the puppy in her bicycle basket and managed to get a sailor to lift the bike off the boat and on to the quay.

She felt elated to have her feet on English soil again.

The last few weeks were behind her as though they had been a nightmare — and yet parts of the dream in France had been strangely pleasant — meeting Geoff, and her time cooking in the French house.

So much had happened to her in the past few weeks. Unbelievable experiences. Her mind was in a whirl thinking about what she'd been through. She wanted to cry with relief that she was still alive, and yet she felt like singing with joy.

But where am I? Where should I go?

Standing around on the quay, with this strangely dazed feeling, and wondering what to do, she was soon told to move on by a military policeman, and so she began to move. Why she felt so incapable of doing anything even though she was safely back in England she couldn't understand. It didn't make sense.

A little nose pushed out of the bicycle basket and the puppy looked at her mournfully.

'Oh, you poor little mite!' she spoke to the pup, 'you've been so good, and just as I promised Bill, my boyfriend who died in Malta that I would look after his dog, I will look after you because you were Fred's little doggie.'

Having taken on the responsibility of Fred's puppy it made her forget her memories of Normandy, and come to her senses.

'Now, what shall we do, Freda?' she asked the little pup as she stroked its head.

A series of whines reminded her that she must feed it.

Getting on her bicycle she rode along the quay and saw a NAFFI mobile van.

A nice cup of English tea was pictured in her mind — and water and some food for the dog.

Having to concentrate on not only her needs, but on Fred's puppy too, made her snap out of her lethargy as she approached the canteen van.

The two women in overalls looked at Vera scornfully when she asked for a cup of tea.

'We don't serve civilians,' one said.

For the first time Vera was aware of how others would see her — a ragamuffin. Her hair had grown over the past few weeks and was longer than she normally wore it. And instead of it being brushed off the forehead and neatly rolled off her collar, it straggled untidily around her face and neck, as it had been blown about in the Channel wind. She hadn't worn any lipstick for ages and her lips were not smooth and kissable.

Her clothes were a mixture of some clothes she'd left home with and some Jeanette had kindly given her, because her bump was beginning to make her skirt too tight around the waist. Her stockings had many runs, and her shoes hadn't seen any polish for ages and were covered with sand.

But that didn't make her feel inferior — in fact she felt quite pleased to think she'd come through all she had, and didn't see why she had to accept being put down by a couple of stay-at-home tea servers.

She propped her bike up against their van and ignoring their contempt she said crisply, 'I've not just biked up from the town to cadge a free cup of tea.' Even mentioning tea made Vera's mouth water, and she was determined to get it.

As neither of them made any move to pour any out for her, Vera went on, 'You might be NAAFI girls serving tea and buns to service personnel. But you are not supposed to shut up shop just because I'm not in uniform. I had to destroy my military identity card in France in case I was captured by the Jerries, and the papers Colonel Parkington, he's my husband, gave me, were kept by a military policeman on the beach at Arromanches.'

'Oh yes?' said one young woman with a giggle, poised with her hand on the huge metal tea pot handle, as she winked at her assistant and said, 'Now tell us another story.'

Vera took a deep breath and tried again.

'I'm the supervisor of British Restaurant s in Norfolk.'

'So, why are you here? We can't serve any Tom, Dick and Harry a free cup of char, just because they happen to be on holiday here at the seaside.'

Vera's face glowered. Her argumentative nature came to the fore. 'Listen you two, just because you can't see any farther than a tea urn, it doesn't mean everyone else does their national service behind the hatch of a NAAFI canteen van. I've just come back from France after doing my duty helping with the invasion. Now don't tell me you can't spare me a cup of tea. Get on the phone to your manageress, Dulcie Swanton or Doreen Thornhill, or Susie Salter, they all know me — Vera Parkington — and they won't refuse me a cuppa.'

The women looked at each other. 'Well, in that case,' said one, 'I suppose we'd better give you one.'

'Well, don't put yourself out too much, will you?'

Looking a little nervous now because of her cross manner, and obvious officer tone as she was used to giving instructions, the girls handed her a cup of tea.

'Mmm, it's lovely. Heavenly,' Vera said, after sipping it.

'Actually it's a bit stewed.'

'You wouldn't notice that if you'd been without tea for weeks. You can't imagine how much I've pined for a cup of tea while I've been in France.'

'Glad you like it. Want another?'

'Thank you, I would — if it's not too much trouble.'

The women's eyes met and they smiled.

'I'll make you a fresh pot, Ducky. Want a bun?'

'If you're sure you can spare it.'

As Vera munched her currant bun — which was probably very ordinary made with wartime ration ingredients, but tasted good to her, she wondered how other men and women returning to England after the war was over would be treated. Would they face the disbelief she'd had to put up with? No-one appreciating just what it was like over there as the troops battling forward across Europe.

She was determined that when, and please God it would be soon, Geoff returned home, she would be far more understanding about the agonies he had suffered.

Feeling better after her refreshment,

she asked the women where the NAAFI quarters were. After they directed her, Vera said, 'Now I have one more waif and stray for you to help.'

The women looked out of the hatch looking for another person. Vera went to her bike and picked up the puppy.

Vera held up the rescued puppy for them to see.

'Ahh!' They immediately showed it more sympathy than they'd given her. And Freda was soon lapping up some water and gulping down a small bowl of food.

'Isn't it sweet?'

A little later, fortified with some fresh tea, and a contented puppy in her bicycle basket, Vera retrieved her bicycle and set off to find the NAAFI headquarters.

Vera Makes A New Friend

Vera soon became lost trying to find the way. The dockland was huge. She was glad she had her bicycle as she pedalled here and there, asking directions from service people she met, who looked at her as if she'd come out of a hedge backwards.

She supposed that before the invasion she would have been carted off as a suspicious person to a top secret location, but now security was more relaxed. And there were so many people wearing different uniforms.

I expect they think I'm a char, come in from the town to clean some offices.

She stopped, finding a patch of nicely manicured green grass for the puppy to stretch his legs. And decided she ought to go inside the Nissen hut marked with nothing more than a notice of letters and figures on it, when she heard marching feet and a loud American voice sounded, 'Lady, you're dicing with death allowing that little beast on the commander's lawn.'

Vera turned to look up at an American pilot speaking to her.

'I won't tell him — and hope you won't,' she replied with a grin.

'I guess not. But I advise you to scram.'

Looking again at him more closely she came to the conclusion that he probably was one of the top brass. If not the Commander himself!

Vera wasn't fazed. 'I'm sorry, sir, to have chosen the wrong spot.'

The officer walked over and crouched down to play with the puppy. 'He's a fine fella.'

'Actually, he's a she.'

'OK then, she's a fine English shepherd dog.'

'Actually, she's a German Alsatian. I'm sure she would have belonged to a German manning the defences in Normandy. I was given her on the beach at Arromanches. I was told the mother and her pups had been killed in the bombing — but this one survived.' Vera added in a quiet voice, 'Actually, the soldier who saved her, died — so I'm looking after her.'

'Well, ma'am, if you don't want her. She can come home with me.'

'To America?'

'Sure. I can take her there.'

Vera looked doubtful. 'The poor little mite. She can't help her nationality.'

'I wouldn't allow her to be harmed because she happens to have belonged to a Jerry. And I can assure you she won't be. My family are from Germany originally. We have a farm in Wisconsin and she'll be fine there.'

Vera thought quickly. She already had two dogs to care for. One belonged to Geoff and the other she was given by her previous fiancé to look after. A dog like young Freda would grow to be big and would take a lot of feeding.

'I've only been looking after this pup for one day, but I love her, and would hate her to come to any harm. Are you sure you can give her a good home?'

'The best. Our family love dogs.'

As a senior officer she knew he would have no great difficulty having Freda shipped to his home.

'Well, I don't know if I should . . . ' the American officer looked fairly old, a reliable gentleman — and he obviously liked dogs.

As she was hesitating he asked, 'Can I give you anything for her?'

Vera hesitated. The Americans had so much more money, food and it was tempting to ask for something. 'No, no. Just look after her, please. And in Fred's memory, call her Freda, will you?'

She felt tears coming into her eyes as she handed the puppy over to the American. But she felt quite sure Freda would have as good a life as he could give her.

She was asked for her name and address so that he could send her a report on Freda. And then the officer gave her the directions to the NAAFI Headquarters.

It was hard to have to get on her bike again and pedal away without the little dog sitting up in her basket.

'Sure you don't want anything?' he called after her.

Vera was so close to breaking down. She dare not stop. She pedalled on but shouted over her shoulder, 'Send me some nylon stockings.'

* * *

It was just as well she knew Dulcie Swanton, and was soon given the help she needed. After a bath in the regulation depth of four inches of water, and a change of clothes — albeit wartime utility quality — and a hair cut, Vera felt more herself. And yet, she knew she was not as she used to be, she'd changed forever.

Tucked away in her heart and memory were all those people she'd met in the last few weeks. Brave people, who had died, or some had survived as she had through one of the most eventful periods of mankind. Each person had their own experiences to talk about, or refuse to talk about because it was too painful for them.

She would be able to share some of her experiences with Geoff when he got home, because she now had some knowledge of the war. And in later years they would be able to tell their child about the wartime they'd experienced.

She was delighted to meet Susie and Doreen again when they came off duty in the evening. Having an evening meal with her, they listened to what Vera told them, with urges to go on and tell more.

Susie said, 'Well, I think you are very brave, Vera.'

'Me? Go on. I merely did what I had to just to survive.'

'And how is Parkie? I mean your husband, Colonel Parkington?'

A cloud came over Vera's face.

'He was well the last time I saw him . . . but he looked as if he'd had . . . '

To her surprise picturing him was too

much for her, and Vera put her hands over her face and sobbed.

'She's exhausted,' said Doreen standing up and putting her arm around Vera. 'Come on, love, we'll get you to bed.'

In a motherly fashion the two NAAFI girls soon had Vera tucked up on a camp bed having given her another nice cup of tea.

'Thank you,' murmured Vera, and went to sleep almost at once.

The two NAAFI girls looked back at sleeping Vera before they switched off the room light.

Susie said quietly, 'I can't imagine what she says she's been through, can you? I can't believe all she said had happened to her was true.'

'I dunno,' whispered Doreen, 'she doesn't strike me that she was making it all up.'

They closed the door and walked along the corridor. Susie commented, 'Well, it's true she's expecting a baby — that's obvious.'

News From Vera's Mum

After arriving home at last, her mother hugged her tightly. 'You've been away for so long. Now tell me about what you've been up to,' Mum said, as the two dogs barked and wagged their tails furiously.

Vera who was dressed in a government utility issue suit, shoes and stockings, took off her battered kitbag and said, 'I got my bicycle mended by a German soldier.'

Mrs Carter looked down at her visible bump and smiled.

Her mother's eyes sparkled, 'I'm thrilled to be a grandmother.'

'You're not quite yet, Mum.'

'No, but I'm going to be. I saw some beautiful knitting patterns for baby clothes in this week's magazine.'

Vera laughed, 'Before you start on them, I need a new cardigan — I left mine in France.'

'Say that again . . . you say you went where?'

Vera put her arm around her mother's shoulders, and said, 'Let's put the kettle on and have a cup of tea. Then I'll tell you all about my adventures in France. I was there for several weeks.'

Blinking, her mum said, 'You might have sent me a postcard!'

It seemed hours later, over several cups of tea, that Vera related her experiences in France. From the humorous moments to the tragedy of lives lost when the invasion began.

'And Geoff?' asked Mum anxiously. 'Where is he now?'

Vera shook her head. 'I expect he is busy. He was elated when they got the floating harbour over to France. And then repaired it after the terrible storm that ripped the American A Mulberry to pieces. But that was his job — where he and the other engineers working with him showed their grit and skill.'

'You ought to be proud of him.'

'Oh, indeed I am, Mum. That dock enabled enormous supplies to get ashore after the initial invasion, until they captured a port.'

'So now Geoff will be coming home?'

'I doubt it! The army will dream up another engineering problem to solve I expect, as the army moves across Europe. I wish that wicked Hitler would give in, but Geoff says the German army is an excellent fighting machine and they're making our soldiers fight all the way ... I'm worried about Geoff.'

Thinking of all the people being killed and injured over there, made Vera put her hands over her face.

'You did your bit, love,' Mrs Carter said, 'Try not to worry too much.'

'At least he hasn't got to worry about me now,' Vera said, looking at her mother with a grin.

'But I'm sure he will be thinking of the mother-to-be.'

'He doesn't know.'

'Vera! Didn't you tell him? Didn't he notice?'

'I don't think so — anyway, he is such a worrier I didn't want him to have to worry about his son too.'

Mrs Carter smiled with her mouth tightly closed.

'You are something else, Vera.' Then feeling her age, she got up stiffly and said, 'Well, we must get on I suppose. I have some ironing to finish and then I'll get us something to eat. And the dogs need feeding and the hens will have to be put to bed.'

'Oh, so you've got some hens in the garden now, have you, Mum?'

'Yes, four. John helped me to buy them and house them. He knows a lot about keeping hens. And I can exchange eggs with friends for other things. And they are laying so will you make us an omelette? No one can make them better than you can.'

Vera looked at her mother with pride. The older lady had to cope with the wartime, just as the service personnel had. Rationing had become even tighter, sometimes things were difficult to buy even if they were on the ration.

'Of course I will. And are there any saladings left in the garden?' she was thinking of the lettuces, tomatoes and radishes that had been planted earlier in the year.

'You may find a few.'

As Vera began to think about cooking again, she began to wonder how her British Restaurants were managing while she was away — and then of course she'd have to arrange for someone to take over her job when she had the baby.

It was all a challenge. But Vera felt so glad to be home. Her only ache was wondering what was happening to her beloved husband in war-torn France.

'John will be popping in to take the dogs for a walk. Can you make an omelette for him too?'

'John?'

'You know John.'

Vera smiled. She sensed that she

would soon learn much more about her mum's neighbour, John Baxter, who'd been helping her with walking the dogs. In her mum's conversation, John was thrown in all the time!

And when the elderly, upright gentleman arrived the dogs went mad to see him.

Struck by his kindly face and the fondness he showed to her mother, as well as the dogs, Vera shook his hand warmly.

'You would never believe half of what Vera's been up to in France,' Mrs Carter said, 'it's just as well I didn't know all about it until she got back safely.'

Vera dismissed her mother's quick account of her experiences, saying, 'I bet John has many stories to tell about his soldiering years.'

Walking with his own dog, plus Vera's two, was quite an art, but the agile ex-soldier was well able to control all three on their leads as they trotted along with him. When John and the dogs set off down the road to exercise in a nearby park, Mrs Carter looked after him, and told her, 'John has asked me to marry him.'

Shocks galore Vera had had in the last few months of her life — but this was a delightful surprise.

'Oh, Mum!'

Mrs Carter studied her daughter's face and asked tentatively, 'Do you think . . .'

Vera hugged her mother, 'It's what you want that matters, Mum.'

'But do you like John?'

'I hardly know him.'

'I said I'd wait 'til you got home, before I made up my mind.'

Vera cried, 'Your happiness is what matters, Mum. Will you be happy married to him?'

Her mother nodded her head. 'I think so, dear.'

'Pity we haven't some champagne to celebrate!'

'Hold on. He only mentioned it. And I said I wanted to wait and think about it. He may not ask me again.'

'Well I'm sure he will — especially as he won't have to take my two dogs for a walk every day.'

★ ★ ★

It was a week later when John had checked over her car to make sure it was still in working order that Vera piled in the car, the dog beds, bowls, and her two dogs with her.

Before she left she thanked John for walking her dogs every day. 'It was very kind of you John. Three dogs to take out couldn't have been easy at times.'

John put his arm around her and gave her a quick kiss on her cheek.

'Vera, love, they were no trouble. It was my war work — and very pleasant to do. I love dogs.'

Momentarily Vera thought of the German puppy, Freda, and hoped she was as well looked after and happy as her dogs were.

John added, 'Anyway, walking the

dogs has given your mum and I the chance to get to know each other.'

Vera smiled.

'I'll miss the dogs. I've got used to them now,' Mrs Carter said.

'You've got John, and his dog.'

Her mother smiled, 'So I have.'

'Anyway,' Vera reminded her, 'next week I'll come over on my day off so we can go shopping for baby things.'

Mrs Carter brightened.

'Mind you,' Vera said, 'new things may not be available to buy. Geoff will understand his son may have to have second-hand things. We'll look in the second-hand shops for a cot and pram. And you get knitting his baby clothes — because I won't have the time.'

'I'd like to do that — it will make a change from knitting socks for soldiers. Which reminds me . . . ' she whispered. 'John has kindly given me some clothing coupons for you to buy a larger size winter coat for yourself.'

Vera put her head on one side and smiled at her mother, and whispered back, 'Isn't that thoughtful of him — I'll have to repay him sometime.'

Soon she was off in her car, with the dogs looking out of the window as she waved to her mother, and John, standing by her on the pavement.

She thought of Churchill's words about an end of the beginning — or was it the start of the end? Well, whatever it was, Vera felt a new chapter in her life was just beginning.

News From Geoff

There was much to do settling back home again. Vera felt she was in a dream as she looked at familiar things and began to sort things out.

Of course there was the ache in her heart that Geoff wasn't there. But there was a letter from him, which she tore open to read.

My dearest Vera,

Intelligence told me you had arrived back in England and I was so relieved to know you are safe.

Fighting continues here and I have been assigned to constructing a river crossing as Mulberry has done its job well.

It is good to know we are winning at last, but the war will drag on because the Germans are determined to fight to the end. I don't have to tell you the horrors that means to so many people. I hope and pray it will all be over soon.

The winter weather is setting in and I long to snuggle down with you.
Your loving,
Geoff.

It took some time for Vera to come down to earth after she'd read his letter. His face was pictured in her mind, and his new worries about other engineering projects he'd been given to do. And with the cold Continental weather, she hoped he was able to wrap up warm.

Feeling a poke on her leg, she looked down to see Battle, Geoff's dog, asking for his dinner. And close behind sat Gyp, Bill's dog, hoping to get his feeding bowl filled too.

Wiping the tears from her eyes, Vera heaved herself up from the armchair where she'd sat to read the letter, and felt her bump.

'Let's hope your father is safe, whatever happens,' she told her unborn child. 'In the meantime, I must get on. There is so much to be done.'

Vera decided keeping herself busy was the best thing she could do, to prevent herself from moping. And knowing women all over Britain were probably doing the same thing as they waited for their menfolk to return, helped her to accept the ache of Geoff's absence.

'Come on then, you rascals,' she said, 'Let's see what I can find for you to eat. And that applies to baby and me as well,' she added patting her tummy.

Whatever lay ahead she thought it was going to be a very busy and exciting time.

She just wished she could hear from Geoff again and know that all was well with him.

Life Returns To Normal

Leaving the dogs with the farmer every day, as Vera usually did when she went off to work, allowed the animals to be with the farm dogs around the farm yard, instead of being locked up in the cottage all day. They were used to spending the day at the farm and were trained not to run off — or chase the farm animals. They had the hay barn to shelter in if they wanted to sleep until she fetched them later in the day.

The farmer wasn't in the least curious to know where Vera had been for the past few weeks. His mind was wrapped around his hectic daily routine of farming, and even with the help of his hardworking Land Girls, he was still left short of male workers because the men had been sent away to join one of the armed forces. But, leaning on his walking stick, he greeted her with his warm smile when she dropped the dogs off.

'We'll keep an eye on 'em,' he told Vera good-naturedly, giving both dogs a hearty pat, as Vera thanked him.

'What's that brainbox husband of yours been up to, then?'

Vera replied, 'Goodness knows!' as she got back into her car. 'I don't like to think about what he's doing — I just want him home again.'

'Has he left you?'

Vera laughed, 'I hope not! But there's quite a fight going on over there in Europe.'

The farmer looked at the peaceful countryside that surrounded him.

'I can't be thinking of that,' he said, 'I have my cows to worry about — and if the weather holds, for the corn to be cut.'

Vera knew farmers' jobs, feeding the nation, was vital war work, so she didn't make any comment about the terrors the fighting soldiers faced. She just said, 'I just pray every day for Geoff to return home safely.'

'Expect you do, Mrs Parkington. Now do you want my lad to start delivering milk to the cottage again?'

'Yes please, and I'll need an extra half pint.'

The farmer touched the rim of his cap, and winked at her.

'Aye, I can see that.'

Vera chuckled and drove off towards Lynn.

* * *

When she arrived at the British Restaurant in Lynn she parked the car and strode into the building.

She was confronted by a gawky woman, dressed in a white overall and her hair covered turban style, who yelled at her, 'Can't you read? We don't open till twelve o'clock.'

Vera was taken aback.

Seeing Vera was not backing out of the door, the dinner lady approached and put her long nose inches away from Vera's.

'Didn't you hear me,' she said, 'we are not open. Wait outside.'

Vera giggled. She was being ordered out of her British Restaurant! The first restaurant she had started over a year ago when it was no more than a hall, with a kitchen attached, that she had had to turn into a mass feeding centre.

Seeing the woman's face becoming furious with her, Vera said hastily, 'Don't panic. I work here, I'm the local supervisor of British Restaurants.'

The woman looked her up and down sceptically, 'Oh yes?'

'Yes. My name is Mrs Vera Parkington.'

It obviously didn't ring a bell with the hostile woman who still seemed determined to throw her out of the building.

A voice from afar called, 'Mabel. Come and give me a hand carrying this basin.'

'Coming,' shouted back the overall

clad woman, 'but I'm just shooing out an early customer who's come in and doesn't want to leave.'

'OK. I'll deal with her.'

Moments later, Margaret Smallwood appeared, and shrieked, 'Vera! Is it really you back at last?' as she rushed in the hall to greet her boss.

Vera was soon ushered into the kitchen and began receiving smiles all round from the dinner ladies. There was elderly Gladys, still doing volunteer war work although in her late seventies. Young Sally, who was now a competent cook and teaching even younger Mary. And Margaret herself, who Vera had known at school as a bossy individual, but because she had become an unwed mother, her career had been changed to cookery — which she soon learned, and had become very competent at organising the restaurant meals after Vera left.

Crowding around her, all the girls wanted to know what she'd been up to.

Vera put her hand over her eyes and sighed, 'You wouldn't believe all I've been through. I went to France.'

'Whatever for?' said Gladys, straightening her cook's cap.

Vera replied, 'I had to get a message to Geoff.'

Mary piped up, 'Couldn't you have sent it by post?'

'No, the Germans wouldn't have delivered it.'

There was a shocked silence.

Margaret asked, 'You mean you went over there?'

'Yes,' said Vera, 'I did.'

Stunned into silence for a moment or two, the girls looked aghast. Then they bombarded Vera with questions.

'Did you see Geoff?'

'Briefly.'

'Ahh! How is he?'

Vera's husband was known and liked by them all when he was the supervisor of the British Restaurants, as a cover for his top secret war work preparing the floating docks for D-Day. Vera had taken over his job as supervisor when he married her. She smiled thinking of him and momentarily hoped he was still OK.

'He was fine. But we all had to keep our heads down at all times — with the Gestapo around.'

Sally's eyes almost popped out of her head.

'You mean the enemy was there?'

Vera laughed, 'Surely you know they took over France, and our Tommies had to shove 'em out on D-Day?'

'Crikey!' exclaimed Sally. 'I don't know how you were in the middle of all that!'

Gladys nodded and said, 'Well, I think that was very valiant of you.'

Margaret snapped. 'Madness, I call it, to have been caught up in all that — it's a wonder you got back in one piece, Vera.'

Vera took in a deep breath and gave a long sigh, 'I sometimes wonder how I made it, myself. Yes, indeed, it seems like a dream now.' And not all of it pleasant she thought looking at her friends' faces all anxious to know all about what she'd done.

'Do tell us about your adventure — we want to know everything, mind.'

Vera said firmly. 'Not now, later, after the meal's over.'

Although it didn't take long for Sally to guess, 'Vera, you're expecting!'

Vera went a little pink in the face. She was hoping to break the news later.

Sally skipped around Vera joyously because she loved babies. Until Margaret barked at her, 'Sally get those biscuits made and put them in the oven. At once!'

With hundreds of hungry customers who would soon be forming a queue outside the hall door, ready to be fed, everyone went back to the jobs they were doing. Vera quickly washed her hands saying, 'What's on the menu, Margaret. Can I give you a hand?'

The activity in the kitchen was abuzz as all the women set to to make up for lost time.

But Vera wasn't surprised that the dinner ladies, all of whom were completely ignorant of cooking for the masses until she had trained them, soon got to work and produced a tasty sausagemeat loaf with vegetables in a parsley sauce, followed by a semolina pudding with some biscuits, a somewhat stodgy meal — but designed to fill empty stomachs.

As Margaret remarked to Vera, 'The food rationing gets worse and worse. Thinking of how to feed everyone becomes more of a headache for every cook these days.'

Although the battles in Europe were going to bring success for the Allies, Vera knew the people at home were being asked to pull in their belts even more. Food shortages were a headache. She sympathised with Margaret.

'You'll be all right, being pregnant. You'll get a green ration book for extra rations,' said Margaret, who'd been through her own pregnancy.

'That'll come in handy,' Vera said, thinking she would have to consult Margaret about a lot of things concerning motherhood.

★ ★ ★

Later, seated around the big kitchen table, after the meal was over and everything cleared away, Vera was just as keen to know their news as they were to hear hers.

Over cups of tea, Mabel was properly introduced and Vera was pleased to find that despite her first impression of the woman was not favourable, Mabel was in fact a valuable addition to the kitchen staff.

Careful not to tell the girls about the most harrowing experiences she'd had, Vera kept them all long after they would normally go home, but at last they had to part and only Margaret remained.

'So, how is little Deanna?' asked Vera when the others had gone.

'She's a right little rascal, running about, into everything,' replied Margaret fondly. 'But her dad helps me to look after her.'

Vera asked cautiously, 'Her dad?'

Margaret shook her head. Vera knew

Margaret's family had cast her out when she'd become pregnant and was not married. The old stigma of unmarried women being sinful was still strong with many people.

Geoff Parkington, who had been to university with Margaret, had helped her find a place to live and had got her a job at the British Restaurant.

'So, he came back?'

Margaret smiled. 'Yes. He said he didn't know I'd become pregnant. And now he's keen to marry me.'

'That's wonderful news!'

Margaret pursed her lips. 'Well I told him I'm thinking about it. You see I suffered so much when he left me and I thought he shouldn't have walked out of my life. I keep asking myself now, does Tom really want me — or Deanna? He loves his little girl.'

Vera could offer her no advice on that query Margaret had. She didn't know Margaret's brother's friend, who Margaret claimed was her daughter's father. She knew the couple must work it out for themselves. So she asked, 'Have you any baby stuff Deanna's grown out of I could use?'

'Sure. I'll look some things out for you.'

Vera poured them another cup of tea, saying, 'I don't want to delay you getting home much longer, but we must just discuss something important.'

Margaret looked at Vera apprehensively.

'I am going to be unable to work, so I was wondering if you would take over my job as supervisor?'

Vera could tell Margaret liked the idea. Being a natural leader, Margaret would be able to do it with no difficulty.

'You'll have to learn to drive, of course.'

'Tom has a car. He'll teach me.'

It was not necessary for new drivers to pass a test when they wanted to drive a car in wartime, so Vera knew that if Margaret wanted to drive — she would.

'Now as for this canteen, I think we should train Sally to take over.'

Margaret huffed. 'She's just a kid.'

'I know, eighteen is very young, but think of all the eighteen-year-olds who are fighting for their country at the moment? And youngsters who have other important jobs. I think Sally will be glad to avoid going into the services. Anyway it would be a waste to see her leave here. If she is made the manageress here she will be able to qualify as having a reserved occupation.'

Margaret, who in the past had had a good deal of lip from as well as fights with young Sally, had to admit that the girl was now very good at the job. Gladys was too old, Mary was too inexperienced and too young, the new woman, Mabel, was as brittle as hard toffee, besides she was too new to know the ropes yet.

'I think Sally will do fine,' said Margaret, 'only you do realise the girl played about at school, consequently she can barely read and write, don't you?'

Vera was not really surprised.

'We'll just have to ask her if she wants the job, and if she does, and she'd be a fool to miss the opportunity, she'll have to give up going out with the boys every night and knuckle down to doing some simple reading, writing and arithmetic. She must be able to read the recipes correctly and the Ministry of Food will expect the stores to be ordered properly and all the paperwork kept up to date.'

'Who's going to tell her that?' asked Margaret.

Vera drank the last drop of tea in her cup. 'I will. I'll have a few weeks before the baby is born and I'll find time to coach her.' She didn't like to add that keeping herself occupied was the best thing as it would prevent her from brooding and pining for Geoff.

Having sorted out her plans for her job being taken over, Vera returned to the farm to fetch the dogs with mixed feelings. So much was going to happen in the next few months. The winter had to be got over. And baby clothes as well as a room had to be prepared for the new member of the family.

Would her mum decide to marry John Baxter, she wondered. And would Margaret marry Tom? And would she and Geoff have a boy or a girl? She must go to the doctor and arrange for a midwife . . .

Then her job had to be prepared for Margaret to take it over. And Sally had to be instructed to enable her to take over Margaret's job.

By the time she got home she was feeling shattered. Carrying around the weight of the baby was tiring.

After parking the car in the barn, she walked around to the front of the cottage and saw on the front doorstep, a package.

Picking it up, Vera was alarmed. It had been delivered by military courier. Who had sent it to her — was it Geoff?

What could be in it?

Vera Worries About Geoff

Tearing off the wrappings of the package, Vera felt some slippery things fall out of her fingers on to the floor. Looking down she was amazed to see several smaller packets.

'What the devil are these?'

She pushed the dogs' noses away, because they were just as curious as she was to see what she'd been sent.

Stooping down, which was now a little difficult for her with her bump, she picked up the fallen packets and spied the words: *Best Quality Nylon Stockings*.

'My goodness!'

Vera was overwhelmed. That American officer who'd taken Fred's puppy had sent her six packets of nylon stockings! She had heard the Americans were generous — but six pairs! She felt like a queen.

Making sure she managed to get them all before the dogs took them off to play with, Vera sank into her armchair with the nylons on her lap with a broad smile on her face — and yet with tears of joy, too. It was such an unexpected gift — a lovely present.

She felt exhausted and kicking her shoes off she closed her eyes and snoozed until Battle, Geoff's dog, poked her leg with his hard nose, reminding her she should get up and feed them. Battle was always ready for his dinner and would devour anything.

It wasn't until later when they had all eaten and she was clearing away before going to bed because she felt too tired to even wait up for the nine o'clock news on the radio, that she noticed a letter had been included with the nylon stockings.

Opening it she almost screamed with delight. There was a photograph of Fred's Alsatian puppy, Freda. It was a lovely close up shot of the young

German Shepherd dog, looking alert with her ears pricked up and showing her beautiful tan and black markings.

The photograph showed Freda in a country area, with the glorious colours of the tree leaves of autumn, called the Fall in America, sparkling in the background.

Freda had certainly fallen on her four feet!

Vera felt so pleased to know the dog had found a good home. Yet Vera continued to weep. Partly because she was thinking of Freda being happy, but also of Gyp, her boyfriend's mongrel, who was well looked after and living with her. And then, Battle, Geoff's Labrador, which, of course reminded her of him.

Geoff, where are you?

Despite her busy days, her pregnancy, which seemed to take all the stuffing out of her, Vera never forgot Geoff for long. She was always wondering how he was — hoping for a letter from him.

It was all she could do to crawl off to bed that night.

★ ★ ★

Colonel Geoffrey Parkington was thinking of his wife too. He kept waiting for some news of her and was becoming more distraught that he didn't have any.

But then, he didn't have the time to write to her either, other than a quickly written message, before he fell on to his bunk bed exhausted each night. He was constantly being expected to work out one engineering problem after another.

Weeks, and now months, had gone by since D-Day and the Germans were still fighting with all the skill and warfare they possessed.

The Allied armies push into Europe was not straightforward.

Dog tired, and dejected, Geoff was able to do his duty, keep his nerve and find answers when called upon to do so, but the longer they found him useful the more the army relied on him for help. Geoff made sure his juniors were given leave, and came back refreshed, but he had none — his senior officers found him irreplaceable. He could have demanded some leave, but he did not.

One morning he staggered when he got up. He'd got a headache. He couldn't eat breakfast and couldn't bear the sound of gunfire and mines exploding around him any longer.

Without thinking he crawled out of the foxhole he was in and walked over to the sick bay, when he heard a whizzing sound overhead.

A terrific explosion, followed by earth thrown up in front of him was all he remembered.

No News For Vera

The winter days were approaching fast. Vera had received another very short message Geoff had written to her, which she thought was curt and uninformative. He didn't say where he was, or what he was doing. Worse, he didn't say he loved her or longed to be with her again. He might just as well have been asking for reinforcements, she told the dogs who sat and listened to her complaint.

And she couldn't reply because she didn't know where to send his mail.

'To Colonel Geoffrey Parkington, somewhere in France, or maybe he isn't there any longer?' she told the listening dogs, who merely wagged their tails.

She sighed as she fingered the crumpled note.

'Well, I expect he's up to his eyes in work and hasn't had any time to do more than scribble this very short message. But I do wonder . . . if he still loves me as much as he used to. Anyway, I have work to do, so it's no good crying over spilt milk.'

Vera was aware that the wives and families of many service personnel were constantly worried about their loved ones, wondering what was happening to them and hoping they were safe. And of those who had received telegrams from the Army to say that regrettably their husbands, sons or daughters had been killed in the conflict.

Vera just hoped Geoff was all right. And she hoped she had not spoilt his love for her by coming over to France with the information she knew he needed before D-Day.

She just longed to know that all was well between them.

But in the meantime she had a lot to do, which was just as well because it prevented her from brooding.

She had to encourage Sally to read and write recipes, and to fill in forms for provisions. And train Margaret to take over her job, although she was quite sure Margaret was well up to the work. Older than Vera, and a natural leader, Margaret was competent, although a little exacting, which didn't make her as popular as Vera had been with the canteen staff in the various British Restaurants they had to supervise.

'I have difficulty thinking of meals to advise the cooks what menus to prepare,' Margaret said one day as she drove along to visit a Restaurant along a country road in the pouring rain. 'Food rationing is becoming more and more impossible to cope with — we can't just give the diners potatoes and carrots every day.'

Vera admitted it had become a serious problem. Competent though Margaret was, she didn't have a lot of imagination. So Vera said, 'Well I'll try and dream up some recipes for you when you take over. There's lots of free food that can be made from looking around the countryside.'

'Such as?'

Vera went into the possibilities of using blackberries from the hedgerows, and field mushrooms, and fallen apples, which anyone could go out and pick to make wholesome recipes.

'Homemade pickles and chutneys are very good with bread and cheese. Of course it takes time to collect and prepare but older children can be helpful.'

'I didn't think how much work was involved when I agreed to do your job.'

Not only was the weather gloomy — so was Margaret.

Vera knew despite her own personal worries she had to buck Margaret up.

'You'll get used to it,' said Vera as cheerfully as she could. 'Anyway, I notice you're much more confident at driving now, aren't you?'

Margaret gave a little laugh.

'Yes, I like it. Tom has been pretty good at teaching me, when he gets the time. And he allows me to use this car of his and his petrol ration.'

'What does Tom do?'

'He's a farmer — in a reserved occupation.'

'Does the farmer want a wife?'

'He says he does.'

Vera waited to hear whether Margaret had agreed to marry him, but she said nothing more about their relationship. After a while she asked, 'Anyway, you and Tom, and little Deanna, seem to be getting on well.'

'Mmm. Yes, we do.'

'Enough to make a happy family?'

'I dunno.'

They had to wait because a herd of cows were blocking the road, as they changed fields — and the cows were in no hurry.

Vera could sympathise with Margaret not knowing whether she should marry a man who had let her down in the past. Vera, herself, had a problem looming ahead in her marriage. She didn't like to tell Margaret how difficult Geoff had been. And how unappreciative he'd seemed when she'd gone to

France. And now she hadn't heard from him for ages ... 'marriage doesn't prevent troubles with men,' she said.

'How's the baby layette progressing?' Margaret changed the subject not wanting to dwell on their men folk difficulties.

Vera smiled, 'The things you gave me are splendid, thank you. Mum helped me to get nappies and the main things sorted out, so now all I want is the baby!'

They both laughed.

And they continued to laugh when they got on to discussing the effort young Sally was making to improve her education — and Sally's dramatic show of exasperation when she found learning difficult.

Margaret explained, 'I asked her to read the recipe the other day and to get the others to prepare what was needed. And you'd never guess what she did. She said that the word, tablespoonful, looked like teaspoonful to her. So all her puddings turned out looking bright pink with too much cochineal in them. And Sally's face was just as bright in colour when she saw the mistake she'd made. She was on tenterhooks when the dessert was served in case anyone complained about them. But they were gobbled up and the children loved the strong colour!'

Vera laughed. 'Well it taught Sally a lesson. I'm sure she'll be more careful to read the recipes accurately in future. But we all make mistakes . . . '

The cattle on the road had moved on and Margaret started the car again. Vera said, 'The good thing is, Sally is working at improving her reading, writing and arithmetic — and in the long run it will pay her to persevere. So encourage her, Margaret.'

'Oh, I do. Although she gets upset after I correct her . . . '

'I'm sure she's only letting off steam because she finds it so difficult. But after the war, when the British Restaurants are closed, Sally will be able to get a job in catering anywhere.'

Margaret sighed. 'Vera, do you think the war will ever end?'

'We are winning. But both the German and the Japanese are resisting, strongly — our soldiers are meeting stiff opposition — it's just a matter of time now before they are defeated. In the new year we will be having a victory parade.'

Margaret merely grunted, 'I hope you're right. How's Geoff's job going?'

Vera didn't like to say anything, but she knew she must.

'Well, his big project went well, but now he is engaged in mending roads and building bridges that were destroyed in the bombing.'

'It must have been awful, being there as you were.'

'It was. A nightmare.' Vera's mind was too full of memories to want to talk about it.

They drove on in silence.

Margaret asked, 'But Geoff is safe now, isn't he? If he's working behind the fighting as the army moves on?'

163

'Yes,' Vera agreed, 'I can only hope he is well behind any danger. He told me before I left him that he was going to build temporary bridges and assist the French to repair damage after the bombing.'

Vera dare not go on to tell Margaret how concerned she was that she'd noticed that Geoff was beginning to show signs of becoming an older man with the huge workload he was being told to do. But she didn't have to because they had arrived at their destination.

Soon the girls were engaged in looking over the kitchen, and inspecting the food being served.

'Plum duff was a good choice for a pudding,' Vera told the cook who beamed to be praised.

The cook said, 'My sister has a small orchard and gave me the plums.'

Vera smiled and said, 'Coming here I was saying to Margaret that the local produce is the best to use if you can get hold of it. And the autumn is the best time of the year.'

She always liked to give some encouragement as well as to point out any lapse in food hygiene she noticed. And as she was instructing Margaret too, she wanted her to be positive when approaching the staff. So she was pleased to hear Margaret ask the cook if she was bottling some beans and fruit.

'Yes, we are,' the cook nodded her head, 'apple rings and salted beans we've done already, and a bee keeper gave us some honey.'

'Splendid!' said Margaret.

Later, driving back home they discussed why the sharing of ideas was important. Everyone was busy and tired in wartime, but a little help from one's friends worked wonders.

'And how's your new dinner lady, Mabel Hind, shaping up?' Vera asked Margaret, not wanting to say that she hadn't been at all impressed by the new woman — but then she didn't have to work with her.

'She's OK.'

'But will Sally manage her?'

'Funnily enough, they get on quite well. Chalk and cheese.'

'Can Mabel keep an eye on Sally's arithmetic, do you think?' Margaret nodded. 'As I say, they seem to get on.'

'Strange that.'

'Well, it isn't because I was told Mabel was thrown out of the RAF as being unsuitable for service life.'

'Oh?'

'I don't know the ins and outs of it, but I understand Mabel has a quick temper. She's not too bad in the kitchen. She's just, well as far as I can see, she's just Mabel.'

Vera knew Margaret herself had suffered from being an unmarried mother at a time when it was frowned on. So it was understandable that however tense Mabel was, Margaret would be sympathetic. And so would dear old Gladys. And young Sally was a cheerful friendly girl who would take anyone under her wing. All together the dinner ladies, although different,

166

worked together well as a team.

Vera was delighted to know the day was successful. Margaret seemed far happier now that she had spent the day learning about the job she was about to take over from Vera, as they arrived back at the farm.

And Vera hoped that there would be a letter to her from Geoff.

Devastating News For Vera

There was a letter waiting for her when she arrived home with the dogs she had collected from the farm. It was in a military style envelope and Vera grabbed it quickly without even closing the front door, and sank into an armchair to read it.

It wasn't from Geoff — but it was about him.

The Ministry of Defence. Regret to inform you . . . Vera's eyes became awash with tears as she scanned the typewritten letter. She wiped the moisture from them as she read on.

Colonel G. Parkington, Royal Engineers . . .

Casualty.

That was the word that stuck in her brain. Geoff had been injured.

She breathed heavily and became aware that the dogs were looking at her with concern. It was remarkable how they knew when she was upset.

It was some time before she could read the letter properly. But when she did, she found she had already gathered the most important information. Geoff had been brought back to England with war wounds, and was in a military hospital.

With a thundering heart Vera knew that for all she had already been through since the war began: losing her first boyfriend, Bill, and the daily hardships wartime brought, as well as her dangerous trip to France and seeing the devastation there — now she was faced with terrible uncertainty about what had happened to her beloved Geoff.

How badly hurt was he?

How long she remained in a trance she didn't know, but she suddenly became aware that the light had gone and she was sitting in darkness. She supposed she'd been asleep. And she hoped the contents of the letter was just a nightmare. But it was not and she had to rouse herself and get on with her duties.

Even the dogs had crouched down and not prodded her to be fed.

Vera, she told herself, shake yourself out of this gloom.

Feed the dogs, feed yourself for the baby's sake — and phone Mum in the morning because it wouldn't be fair to phone her before she went to bed so that she would be worrying all night long.

Having settled her mind about what she had to do, Vera got up and went about her tasks like a robot.

She slept well because she'd had a busy day, and carrying the heavy baby around was tiring.

★　★　★

In the morning she looked out on a sprinkling of snow covering the land-scape around the cottage. Blimey, snow before Christmas!

She had to phone the Ministry of Defence and find out about Geoff. Where he was and what injuries he'd suffered.

Having let the dogs out and made herself eat a little breakfast, she was trying to find the courage to make the phone calls when she heard whistling outside. The boy delivering the milk was ladling out her milk from the churn into her can.

★   ★   ★

'Morning, Mrs Parkington,' he said when she opened the door to pick up the fresh milk, 'sorry if I woke you up.'

'Oh, you didn't. I've been up for ages. What are the roads like?'

'Slippery. Don't you go out, missus.'

'No I won't, Jim. Will you tell your dad I won't be bringing the dogs over to him today, please?'

The fifteen-year-old boy gave her a wide grin and hopped back into his cart flicking the horse's reins so that they moved off, with him whistling loudly enough for it to be heard for minutes after he'd left the cottage grounds.

She took a deep breath and phoned her mother.

'Mum, I want you to sit down.'

'I am sitting down. What's the matter?'

'It's Geoff. I've heard he's . . . ' Vera could hear her mother catch her breath as she waited for her daughter to tell her the news. 'Geoff's been hurt. Injured.'

'Oh, I am sorry! What is it?'

Vera realised her mother wanted to know about Geoff's injuries and she thought she should have phoned the MOD first and found out. But she just wanted to share her grief that he had been injured, to get some support and comfort from her mother first.

But was anyone comforting Geoff at the moment?

'Mum, I don't know what he has suffered yet. I ought to have found out . . . '

'Yes, love, you ought to be told. I wish I could be with you.'

Vera wanted to be with her mother too, but she mentioned the snow and ice on the road and they both agreed it would not be wise for her to visit today.

'Vera,' her mother said, 'I think if his injuries were life-threatening you would have been called to his bedside.'

'I suppose so. Anyway, I'll ring again when I know something more about him.'

Ringing off, Vera then plucked up the courage to ring the military number, and after a while she got through to a senior doctor who told her that Geoffrey Parkington was being transferred to another hospital and that she should ring them in a couple of days when they had had time to assess him.

'But can't you tell me what his injuries are?'

'His wounds were minor. But, well you must understand that he has suffered from the blast . . . mentally.'

Vera closed her eyes. She knew

173

nothing about the mental scars of war. How they would affect him — and her.

The doctor was continuing to talk, 'You will have to come and see him. The doctor in charge of his case will explain things to you.'

'Yes,' said Vera woodenly, 'I expect he will.'

'Mrs Parkington.'

'Yes?'

'I've seen far worse cases than his. I'm sure he will recover. But it's a slow process and will require a lot of patience from you.'

'Thank you, Doctor.'

In her shocked state, Vera put down the phone and waited until she'd made herself a cup of tea, and with a shaky hand she drank it. She longed to rush to the hospital and see Geoff. But it was impossible.

She hadn't the petrol to make the long car trip down to the south coast. Anyway, the roads were not safe for travelling. And her baby was due before long. No, she couldn't possibly go and see him. She would have to ring the hospital where Geoff was and explain.

Next, she rang her mother again and told her.

Sympathetic, and as concerned as she was, Mrs Alice Carter was not the kind of person to see the worst of the situation.

'As the doctor told you, Vera, he will get better, I'm sure. In the meantime he is being looked after and you have his child to think about, don't you?'

Vera certainly had. She began to wonder how long she would have to wait until the child was born.

'Yes, Mum,' she said, trying to sound more cheerful than she felt at that moment.

She was excited about the coming birth — yet apprehensive too, as it was her first child.

Margaret too, had to be told that she wouldn't be coming into work. Vera was pleased to think that their previous day together had been worthwhile and she didn't have to worry about the continuation of the job she was leaving.

Now only the future had to be met with courage. The future for her, and her mentally suffering husband, and their war baby — which she felt was due soon.

'We Called It Shell Shock'

Her mother was more concerned about Vera than she'd let on. She went down the road to talk to John about it.

'Come in, Alice,' John said, as he ushered her into his sitting room, 'you shouldn't have gone out on these slippery pavements. You could have fallen over.'

Alice bristled. 'I might be a grand-mother soon, but I'm not that decrepit.'

'No, no you are not. But you could do without a broken arm or leg, m'dear.'

They were a companionable couple and as they sat either side of the fire, and John's dog came nestling up for a stroke or two, Alice told him about the news she'd heard from Vera.

'We called it shell shock in the First World War,' John said. 'I reckon most of us in the firing line suffered from it to some extent.'

'You didn't.'

'Yes, I did. I wasn't as crippled by it as some men were who came home from the front. But I suffered all right. Battle scars made me feel numb and gave me nightmares. But I was all right after a while. Some ex-soldiers' problems took far longer to heal and a few never recovered. When these men got home they took to drinking too much and many marriages were affected.'

Alice shuddered as she sat, stroking the dog's ears and stared at the small coal fire they were allowed in wartime.

'I don't like Vera being on her own,' she said, 'and her baby is due soon — in fact anytime now.'

'Mmm. I'm sorry I can't offer to run you over to her cottage. I haven't the petrol. But I'm sure Vera being such a sensible girl will have made some arrangements for the birth.'

'Yes, she has asked for an ambulance to take her to hospital when her time is near. And the farmer will take care of her dogs until she is able to cope with them again. It's just that being her mother . . . ' her voice wobbled, 'I just want to be there, with her, at this very hard time for her.'

'Of course you do.' He looked across at Vera's mother with understanding.

Suddenly sitting up straight in his armchair he said, 'I tell you what. We can get you a taxi over to her cottage. It will cost the earth, but you'll both be far happier being together, won't you?'

Alice looked at John with a smile.

'You're such a kind man.'

Having to pack and phone for a taxi, was far better for Alice than moping and wondering what was happening to her daughter.

Later that day, Alice, muffled in her coat, hat, gloves and scarf, with her suitcase, knitting bag and spare spectacles — and stone hot water bottle in case Vera didn't have one, was bundled into a taxi.

'Now don't you worry, Alice. I'll cancel your milk and newspaper.'

'John, dear, look after yourself.'

'You too, Alice. And give my love to Vera.'

' 'Course I will.'

Being driven over to the cottage gave Alice time to calm herself, as she looked out over the snow white countryside. A hard frost had made the earth look dead. Trees, leafless and lifeless.

It was, Alice thought, a time for nature's long sleep.

The earth was recovering, and would burst out with fresh young growth in a few months' time.

And by that time Alice hoped many other good things would happen.

'You Haven't Visited Him'

Vera was naturally delighted to see a taxi draw up and her mother being helped out of the car by the driver.

As the dogs barked, Mrs Carter made sure she had all her bits and pieces taken into the cottage, while the driver folded the rug that had been over the lady's legs to keep them warm during the journey, before he waved and headed back to Lynn before it became dark.

'I feel as if a huge weight has been taken off my shoulders,' exclaimed Vera, kissing her mother again.

Mrs Carter's eyes looked at her daughter's huge belly and smiled as she said, 'It won't be long before you have another weight shifted off you,' she said.

Stroking her bump, Vera said, 'I'll be glad when it's all over now. He is really getting in my way now.'

'You think it's going to be a boy, then?'

'Well, I hope so because then he will have his own new clothes and won't have to keep wearing Deanna's cast offs.'

Over a cup of tea they had much to discuss. And soon the conversation got around to Geoff's condition.

'I worry about him, I really do,' said Vera.

Her mother cupped her hands in her face and murmured, 'Of course you do, love. I think you have every reason to be worried. That's why I came to be with you. To see you through this bad patch.'

'Do you think,' Vera stroked the rim of her cup with her finger thoughtfully, 'Geoff will be different?'

'Oh yes, he's bound to be after what he's been through. And so of course will you be, becoming a mum. You'll have to renew your marriage I expect as things may be quite different.'

'What if Geoff doesn't love me anymore?'

'Don't worry about that now. The hospital are looking after him at present and I doubt if you could do any better for him. When you've had your baby and he is coming home you can see how he is, and decide how you can help him. You'll be given some advice from the doctors, I'm sure.'

Vera's teeth went over her bottom lip. She didn't want to succumb to talking about what effects his war injuries might have on Geoff in the long term.

She had her baby due to arrive — and her mum was with her — which was the best possible comfort she could have.

★ ★ ★

'It's a boy!' Vera's hands covered the tiny body placed on her chest as great relief and tiredness overwhelmed her.

She and Geoff had a son.

The midwife was a no-nonsense type of nurse, but for Vera's first experience of childbirth, she'd given her all the benefit of having delivered hundreds of babies into the world.

Vera's labour was over. Seeing her baby son was a great joy. But there was something important lacking in the completeness of her happiness. Her husband was far away and he should be rejoicing too.

'Have you decided on a name for your baby?' she was asked.

She'd given it some consideration. She really hoped to consult Geoff, but before she'd gone into labour she'd been unable to see him and ask him. The winter weather made it impossible for her to travel by train to visit him in hospital. And the petrol was not available to go by car. So she had to make up her own mind what to call the child.

'Victor,' she replied.

Victor was Geoff's second name, and she liked it. The child had been born at a time of victory for the Allied forces in Europe. Not that they had beaten the Germans yet, but the outcome would be, as Geoff had told her after D-Day, just a matter of time.

But she still had heartache over Geoff. Still no news of his recovery from being caught in a bomb blast.

Her mother was ecstatic at the birth of her grandson — and so were Geoff's hotel owning family when they knew. It was a pity they were all living so far from each other they couldn't rejoice together as a family.

Nevertheless, Vera was grateful of her mother's presence and practical help with looking after her and her child when they got back to the cottage. Keeping the mother and infant warm and washing and drying clothes and nappies wasn't the easiest chore in an old cottage with only one fire in the range to keep the place warm.

★   ★   ★

As Vera's strength returned she was able to take over cooking meals for them, trying to give her elderly mother more chance to rest.

'Whew! I had no idea having a child would involve so much work,' she exclaimed.

'This harsh winter weather doesn't help matters,' Mrs Carter said as she arranged some nappies over a clothes horse near the fire.

'Sit down, Mum, I'll finish that job.'

'I think I can hear Victor crying, you'd better go and see to him.'

It was relentless looking after a baby with wartime restrictions — just one difficulty after another.

How she would have managed without her mother's help Vera just didn't know. And John too, came over to the cottage with some provisions he'd managed to collect for them.

But the pleasures were there too. The child was thriving. And Vera was enjoying being able to run up and down the cottage stairs again.

Only her worry about Geoff kept her from being entirely happy. She desperately wanted him back with her and Victor.

Her contact with the hospital where Geoff was remained as formal correspondence. Vera received a few medical reports on his condition, but Geoff stayed too far away for her to visit with her newborn. Trains crammed full of soldiers and with no heating, made it unwise for a mother with a baby to travel.

Apart from that Hitler was now sending bombs that exploded over the London area and no-one knew where they might land.

'How I wish this hateful war would end,' Vera said as she rocked her baby in her arms. 'And it's about time you met your father, young man. He is a very brave man, a very clever engineer, you will be proud of him when you grow up.'

Holding the shawl-covered baby she looked out of the cottage window and sighed. She could see the first signs of spring appearing. The sun was out shining over the countryside like a healing balm. Opening the door, the dogs bounded outside first as she walked out on to the grass and spotted a few daisies underfoot. Yes, spring had come.

Vera continued to talk to her son. 'The days are longer, nature is waking up, and so must I.'

Victor gurgled.

'It won't be long before you'll be out in the garden getting up to mischief.'

His little face formed into a beaming smile.

'So, time has passed by and I must get to see Geoff now. Whatever condition he is in he has had enough time to get better and I must bring him home.'

There were many arrangements to be made before she could leave, and she was so grateful to John who offered to take her to the hospital after collecting as many petrol coupons as was necessary to allow him to get there and back.

★ ★ ★

'Heavens above!' declared Vera, looking at the bespectacled Army doctor sitting opposite her on the other side of his large desk. 'Of course I don't expect my husband to be exactly as he was when I married him. A lot of water had gone under the bridge since then. But I do understand what it is like to be in a bombing raid.'

'Not in the heat of battle you don't, Mrs Parkington.'

'Excuse me, Doctor. I was in France — in Normandy — when the invasion took place. I can assure you we were bombed. So I do know what it is like.'

The doctor's eyes glistened behind his spectacles.

'Hasn't Geoff told you I was there?'

The doctor leant forward making a pyramid with his fingers.

'No. He doesn't think he has a wife. After all, you haven't visited him.'

Vera exploded, 'How could I? I have just given birth to our child. How could I get down here to see him? Why didn't you have him moved nearer to our home so that I could? And his parents are unhappy they are not able to visit him either. It's not that Geoff is not loved. It's this wretched war that keeps us apart!'

The doctor regarded her sympathetically.

'I'm sorry, Mrs Parkington. Because the colonel has been so unresponsive it has been difficult for me to know about your circumstances.' He looked over his shoulder at the bookcase filled with patients' files. 'We have so many mentally ill soldiers to deal with.'

Vera calmed down. She could see his difficulties. He was overworked with many cases needing his care and attention, as well as Geoff's.

'I haven't much time to see him,' said Vera, 'I must get back this evening . . . what advice can you give me?'

'Really, I have none. Every patient is different. They cope with their trauma in different ways. They all need a different amount of time for their minds and bodies to get over the injuries.'

'He's had that.'

'It can take months — years.'

Vera swallowed.

'Then I'd better see him. I have made arrangements to take him home.'

The doctor looked down at Geoff's file and after leafing through some papers, closed the file and said to her, 'It may be the best thing for him. If you feel you can manage to help him over the rest of his convalescence. You will need to be patient with him. But I think you are a sensible woman — a brave woman.'

* * *

She wasn't feeling at all brave when they left the office and began to walk down a long corridor where she noticed men in dressing gowns, some with bandaged heads, arms or legs, sitting and staring into space.

'I've put him in here,' said the doctor, 'so you can have some privacy.' He knocked and then opened the door for

Vera to see a tall man sitting by the window.

'I've brought your wife to see you, Colonel Parkington.'

Geoff, she recognised, as he turned his head to face her slowly.

Her heart beat rapidly — he'd become grey-haired. His cheeks were sunken and there was no sparkle in his eyes.

'I haven't a wife,' he said with no emotion, 'she was killed.'

'I'll leave you,' said the doctor slipping out of the door.

Vera brought another chair to sit by her husband. And for a while she looked at him with compassion as he looked away from her.

'Geoff,' she said, 'It's me, Vera.'

He turned to look at her again, and for a moment she thought he recognised her. But there was no other sign that he knew her.

'Vera was killed,' he said dreamily.

'No, she wasn't!'

He started. 'Who are you?'

Vera took his large hand and stroked it.

'I'm Vera, the woman who loves you dearly. I've come to take you home.'

'I haven't a home — I haven't anything — only pain.'

'What about your dog, Battle?'

'Oh yes, I remember now.' His face showed his kindly expression was still there — part of him. 'Is he still alive?'

'Of course, and Gyp. Both dogs are waiting for you to take them for a walk in the countryside around the cottage as you used to.'

'I'd like that. But I've got a bad foot.'

Vera looked down at his slippered feet.

'Show me. It doesn't look injured.'

He removed his slipper and there was his unscathed foot.

'There, see, it has been mended. You can walk, Geoff.'

He was looking at his foot and wriggling his toes and she longed to kiss him. She longed to kiss his lips, to feel his arms around her after being parted from him for such a long time. But she could tell it was going to take some time to bring him back to normal.

'Nurse,' he said suddenly, 'what's the time?'

She took a deep breath in and said, 'I am not a nurse. I'm Vera. Your wife. Now, listen to me carefully, Geoff. You must understand that I got back to England safely after I left you in France. I am living at our cottage and I want you to come home with me today.'

His eyes penetrated hers.

'Are you really my Vera?'

'Of course I am. Your cook. Remember what a good cook I am?'

'Vera was a good cook,' he muttered, 'a very good cook.'

'Would you like me to cook you your supper tonight? You look as if you need feeding up.'

His face broke into a wry smile.

'Yes. The meals here are awful.'

She laughed gently as she bent over to kiss his worn face.

He seemed to come alive.

'Vera, is it really you?'

'Really,' she replied, kissing him again on the lips.

It was as if a load had been lifted from his shoulders. He took her hand and kissed it.

'Vera, please take me home,' he said.

The doctor was clearly amazed to find them talking and even chuckling together when he called in later.

'Can he come back with me?' Vera asked anxiously.

'Certainly, although don't be surprised if he has a relapse. He might crawl back into his shell again.'

Vera was told he hadn't any belongings, only funnily enough he had his slide rule which he happened to be carrying when he was injured.

'It's important for him to keep that. It may help him to remember those parts of his life that lay buried still.'

Vera thanked the doctor, but was aware the busy medical man had other cases he had to deal with and was not reluctant to let Geoff leave the hospital.

A Difficult Time At Home

She felt triumphant to be bringing him home with her. Although she didn't know what to expect when he had got home — and met his son.

She rang her mother to say she should expect them.

In the back of John's car they sat close together. Sharing the warmth of their bodies. Holding hands, and saying very little.

Mum came up trumps when they reached the cottage, she had left a slow cooking casserole in the range. The dogs went wild having their master home, and Geoff seemed to recognise them.

But he didn't seem at all happy to find a baby in the house.

'Whose baby is it?' he asked when he heard the child cry.

'Mine,' Vera said, then wished she'd said, 'Ours.'

How she wished now she'd told him she was expecting his baby in France. She'd expected Geoff to be thrilled to find he had a son. But he seemed unmoved. Unwilling to accept the child as his.

After Victor was asleep in bed, Mum told Vera that she thought it wise not to tell Geoff that the child was his. 'Let Geoff settle first.'

Vera said, when Geoff had gone upstairs to bed, 'Geoff's coming out of his illness, the doctor told me. We must carry on as normal and let him find his feet. The only thing I think we should do is to tell him repeatedly that Victor is his son.'

Vera almost wept when she got in bed beside him and he ignored her. The whole day had been harrowing. But she succeeded in bringing her husband home — if only he would recognise her as his wife, and Victor as his son.

The Old Geoff Returns

'John has offered to take me home today,' Mrs Carter said in the morning as they were eating their breakfast in the kitchen. 'He thinks, and I think too, you ought to be left together as a family to sort your lives out.'

Vera smiled and said, 'I think we are not the only couple to have to sort our lives out.'

Mrs Carter smiled as she spread some homemade marmalade on her toast.

'Yes, Vera, I've decided to marry John. Do you mind?'

Vera got up from the table and ran around to hug her mother.

'I'm delighted for you. I think John will make you a splendid companion. He's such a good, kind man.'

'Thank you, Vera,' said John coming into the kitchen and overhearing her praise of him. And Vera was delighted to see that Geoff came in behind him too. They had been out walking the dogs together in the early morning sunshine.

Vera longed to embrace Geoff, but he didn't seem to want to show her any affection. Outwardly, he was physically well, but she knew inside his mind was still in turmoil. She would have to be patient.

'Come and have some bacon and eggs,' she said, her mind on her cooking, 'and take your muddy wellies off, you men, if you please.'

It seemed very quiet later that day after her mum and John had left the cottage.

Vera had plenty to do looking after her baby with no-one to help her, because Geoff continued to treat the child as someone else's.

★　★　★

Vera missed her mum's companionship because Geoff kept himself to himself.

He even moved into the spare room.

Every day, although he took the dogs out which did him good, he simply sat around the cottage.

Victor was a good baby but there were times when she wished his father would pick him up and cuddle him because she had more to do now her mother had gone, and found she had less time to play with Victor.

Gradually Geoff began to potter around the house and garden. He began to look at his papers, and sometimes asked her the strangest things. But she was patient and answered his questions until he was satisfied.

They might appear to others to be a contented family, but they were not united. If Geoff did not accept that Victor was his son, and continued to sleep in the spare room, their marriage was ruined.

And as the weeks went by, she began to despair of having him truly back with her.

Her toothache came on suddenly one

day. Vera tried to ignore it at first, hoping it would go away. She was too busy to go to the dentist, but as the pain persisted and got worse, she knew she had to go.

'I have to go to the dentist,' she told Geoff who was cleaning his shoes. His army habits persisted which was a good thing because he was a good-looking man, and he kept himself well turned out, although many of his jackets had patches on the cuffs and elbows.

'Brown's a good chap,' Geoff said.

'I have to go today.'

'Toothache?'

Vera nodded. 'I'll ring and make an appointment.'

Having arranged to go that afternoon — by bus because they had no petrol for the car — she was getting the baby's carry basket ready when Geoff said, 'Leave the baby here. You can't take that big baby basket on the bus by yourself. I'll look after him.'

Vera gulped. Was it wise to leave Victor behind? She said, 'The dental reception nurse will look after him, I'm sure.'

He sounded his old commanding self when he retorted, 'I'm quite capable of looking after a baby for a few hours.'

'I hope I'm not going to be that long.'

Geoff came up close to her and looked into her eyes.

'Trust me,' he said.

He'd guessed her dilemma — was he well enough to act as a nanny for a while?

She had to make up her mind. Could he care for a baby he thought was not his own? Should she show him that she thought he was recovered enough to look after Victor — would her decision help him to feel he was getting better?

'Yes, of course I trust you,' she said decisively.

He lowered his head to kiss her lightly on her cheek and to brush her hair tidy with his fingers.

'I'd like you to get me a few things while you're in town.'

Doing a bit of shopping would make

a nice break. She would be able to get a few things for herself too. Although they were well provided with basic foodstuffs there were other things she'd been meaning to get from town, spices for cooking and some hair shampoo, when she had the opportunity to get there.

'Write a list of what you want and I'll do my best,' she said hurrying to put on her coat, hat and gloves before she changed her mind. 'Victor's sleeping at the moment, when he wakes pop him into his play-pen with his toys, and give him a drink of milk and a rusk to nibble.'

'Am I allowed one too?'

Vera smiled. 'Only one each,' she replied. This was the first time he'd shown his sense of humour she knew of old. It was so good to hear she went back and kissed him on the lips, then rushed out of the cottage with a wide grin on her face, calling back to him, 'I must dash or I'll miss the bus.'

★　★　★

Having the tooth pulled was unpleasant, but the dentist assured her it was necessary. But having the pleasure of shopping — even with a sore gum, allowed her to forget it as she scurried around Lynn, collecting the things on Geoff's list and searching for her own requirements. Especially as the wartime shops looked drab and so many things were on ration.

'Here's a nice pre-war shampoo,' said the chemist's assistant quietly showing it to Vera so that no one else would see. 'I found some in the storeroom the other day when I was tidying it up. I want to offer it to my regular customers, and you and your mum have been shopping here for years.'

'Thanks,' whispered Vera, paying for the bottle and quickly putting it into her shopping bag so that no other customer could see it. 'It'll make me all glamorous like a film star!'

'Your husband will like that. And how's Mr Parkington — the Colonel, I mean?'

'He's getting on fine. He's looking after our little son, Victor, which reminds me I should be getting back. The bus leaves in ten minutes.'

She would have liked to have had the time to pop into the British Restaurant and see the girls, but she didn't want to have to wait another hour or so for a later one. And seated on the bus, she began to be worried about little Victor — was he all right with Geoff?

And then she began to wonder what Geoff would do when he was demobbed from the army, as he would be after his serious injuries. What job could he do? What would he like to do?

She could continue in the catering trade. Cooking was her art. She would have to think where she could work when the war was over — and it did seem, listening to the BBC News that the war in Europe would be over soon. Of course there were still the Japanese to beat, but the Americans were making good progress on that front.

So engrossed in her thoughts, Vera

almost missed her stop and had to get up quickly with her packages and press the bell for the driver to stop.

He did stop a little after the proper bus stop because Vera was so slow telling him that she wanted to get off. And she had to walk back about a quarter of a mile.

The dogs were the first to greet her and she thought it a pity they couldn't carry her shopping.

* ★ ★

By the time she got back to the cottage she felt exhausted. Kicking her shoes off by the front door, and taking off her outdoor clothes, she listened.

There was no sound of Geoff — or the baby.

Panic rose in her chest as she looked around.

Then she spied Geoff sitting in his armchair with Victor in his arms. He was cuddling him and talking to his tiny son. 'Now I consider that very careless of your mother to go and miss the bus, don't you, Victor?'

The child looked up fearlessly into his father's eyes and dribbled as he put his small thumb in his mouth.

Together they made a beautiful picture of father and child, and for Vera it seemed that having to look after the child had allowed Geoff to get in touch with his emotions again. Because he'd nothing to explain to the baby, or the dogs, about his wartime fears and worries, they accepted him as someone who loved them — as they loved Geoff. His past troubles and injuries were over, all that concerned them was the future.

Geoff went on, 'We'll have to train her to do better than that. One rusk is not enough to keep us men going for long is it?'

Tears formed in Vera's eyes. It was plain to see that Geoff was happy with his child — and Victor was happy too. Overjoyed, she called, 'I'm sorry. I forgot to ring the bell to tell the driver I wanted to get off, and he kindly stopped farther on, and I had to walk back.'

As he looked at her, Vera felt embarrassed to have wet eyes and turned abruptly saying, 'I'll put the kettle on. What do you fancy for your supper?'

'Trust a woman to think of an excuse to be late,' she heard Geoff say.

A little later he called to her, 'We want to know if your tooth's OK?'

'Gone,' she replied, from the kitchen as she put the shopping on the table calling back so he could hear, 'Now I hope I've managed to get all the things you wanted. I found some catgut — but what on earth you want that for I can't think.'

He rose and put the baby back into his playpen then came in behind her saying, 'Thank you for getting it,' and picked up the packet containing the string set. 'It's for my violin.'

'I didn't know you had a musical instrument.'

'Well, I have. It's somewhere in the loft.'

'Well I never! So are you going to entertain us?'

'I'll have to get it restrung at first. Then I'll make sure you are out when I start practising.'

'Oh thanks,' Vera said, imagining the unpleasant sounds that a violin could make until it was tuned properly. 'If that's what you want, go ahead.'

'Vera, all I really want, is you.'

She loved the feeling of his arms firmly around her, thrilled that his emotions were returning, and asked, 'and you want Victor too, I hope, now that you've become acquainted?'

He kissed her neck and held her so close she had to beg to be released to be able to make the tea as the kettle started boiling, gushing white steam.

'Of course, Victor too,' he assured her. 'Now get on with making our tea, if you please.'

He sounded like the real Geoff again and she realised a great hurdle in his recovery had been overcome.

A Guest Arrives

Things suddenly seemed to Vera to happen rapidly. First, the newsreader could barely hide his emotion as he read the news telling all those listening around their radios that the war in Europe had come to an end.

After all the heartaches, the losses and privations, a joyous feeling swept the land. The church bells rang and people smiled at each other. Four grim war years were over, and so many things in Britain had changed. And although victory over the Japanese still had to be won, it seemed right to celebrate the conquering of Hitler and all the evil he'd caused.

'Of course, it won't increase our bread rations,' Vera told her baby who just laughed and gurgled at her. 'But by the time you are old enough to want some sandwiches young man, there should be as much as you want to make you grow into a strong man like your father. And the bakers won't bake the awful grey stuff they call bread these days. No, you'll have the lovely white bread the bakers made before the war.'

Victor was now six months old and thriving. Like his father, who'd thrown over his injuries and was becoming his normal self again. He'd taken up playing the violin. Vera didn't particularly like hearing the violin, neither did the dogs, but Victor seemed to like it.

And as Geoff practised and became more competent, he joined a small musical group in Lynn. They met together for musical evenings. All the musicians liked it when they met at the cottage because Vera always managed to make them some delicious refreshments.

'How does your wife manage to make such lovely things to eat?' they asked Geoff.

'She is a marvellous cook — why else do you think I married her?'

Vera grinned at everyone enjoying eating her food — and got her own back by telling them that their planned concert at the local gaol was unfair on the prisoners because they were a captive audience!

Now Vera faced another challenge. She had a Victory Feast to prepare.

She'd been asked by Margaret to be in charge of the British Restaurant's grand party for hundreds of people who planned to celebrate VE Day at the restaurant. The tables would spill out into the street, and the children were wild with excitement as for many it was to be the first party in their lives.

But Vera had to conjure up a memorable feast for everyone — with war rations!

'I can't possibly do it!' Vera cried, throwing down her pencil as she was trying to work out some recipes at home.

'Yes, you can,' retorted Geoff, putting down the newspaper and getting up he walked over to the table to sit with Vera.

'If I can help build Mulberry, then you can feed the five hundred!' He put his large hand over hers and squeezed it gently.

Encouraged, Vera turned to lift her face to kiss him saying, 'You're right. I shall do it — somehow.'

It helped when she received a surprise parcel of tinned food from the American Army Store, sent by Freda's owner, with more photos of the grown dog and Vera was able to explain to Geoff why she'd taken the puppy over to England, and tell him about the American officer who had offered to look after Freda.

But she had the feeling Geoff didn't like the idea of her having a secret American friend — was he jealous? Or maybe he thought she'd had an affair with him, and that Victor was his child? Surely not!

Anyway, the extra tins of American meats and fruits were most welcome to help her organise the food for the party.

A Time For Celebration

On the day before the party she went into Lynn again to discuss the preparation of the food with the girls at the British Restaurant.

Seeing Mabel she said, 'I hope you're not going to try to kick me out of the building this time!'

Mabel grinned. 'Come on in, Vera, I'll get you a cup of tea.'

Having helped the girls clear away the pots and pans, after the midday dinner, they all sat around the big kitchen table.

'And how is little Victor — I'm dying to see him again.' Sally, who loved babies, wanted to know everything she could about him, and Vera, being a proud mum, was happy to give her all the details — until Margaret interrupted.

'How's Geoff?'

Vera's face became serious. 'Well, he's improving. Slowly.'

'Not back to his old self?'

'Not entirely. He still has a little way to go yet.'

Sally asked, 'Will he always be mentally ill?'

Margaret scolded Sally. 'You shouldn't have said that!'

Vera put up her hands and looked at both women.

'Margaret, Sally is only saying what you all must want to know. So I can tell you that he is recovering well from his war wounds. Both physically and mentally you wouldn't really know what he had suffered now . . . but . . . '

She swallowed, not able to tell them that two major difficulties remained that spoilt their relationship. That they were still in separate rooms and that Geoff, although he obviously loved Victor, did not recognise that he was his son.

All the girls were looking at her intently.

A lot had happened to her in the past year. Vera felt she had changed, from being a bride annoyed that her husband was so untidy and harassed about his work, to a woman who had tasted the war first hand.

She'd seen death and destruction — and also she'd given birth to a beautiful boy and was now a seasoned mum. Seeing everything in perspective, she could say, 'It is difficult for me to explain exactly how Geoff has still to overcome all of his dreadful injuries, but I hope and pray that he will continue to improve, and soon he'll be able to work again.'

'Will he stay in the army?'

'No. I think he'll choose something else to do.'

'Is he capable of taking on something new?'

Vera knew that they were only questioning her because they liked her husband and wished him well. She smiled, 'Well, he's taken up playing the violin.'

She was aware of the hushed silence around her.

'Colonel Parkington a fiddler?' Sally was always the first to express what everyone thought.

Vera laughed. 'Yes, much to the horror of my ears at times, he has taken down the violin he played at school and now plays with a musical group once or twice a week.'

'I think that's wonderful!' said Gladys, the kindly volunteer lady, who should have gone home hours ago but wanted to stay and see Vera.

Vera looked at Gladys, who had been one of her first helpers when she started the British Restaurant, and gave her a special smile.

'I think so too, Gladys. Even though I admit at times his scraping makes me want to scream. But Victor loves the racket.'

'Will he come and play at the party?' little Mary wanted to know. 'I'd love to see Colonel Parkington again.'

'Yes, yes,' the girls agreed. 'We all

love him — he's so handsome.'

'He looks just like the film star, Gregory Peck.'

Vera smiled wryly. 'I'll ask him — although you may be sorry you asked him when you hear him play!'

'He won't play that dreary classical stuff, will he?' Sally asked making a face.

Vera assured her that he would be sure to choose some light music for the party.

'Anyway the reason we are here is to discuss the food for the party tomorrow so we'd better get on with it, or there'll be nothing for the party goers to eat.'

Everything was considered and a decision made about who was going to make what from the list of sausage rolls, jam tarts, iced buns, jellies, trifles, ginger cakes, oaty biscuits and dozens more dishes to make the feast memorable.

By the time the meeting broke up, Vera had managed to convince them all that the food could be fun to make — and that there wouldn't be more than a few crumbs for the birds left when the party was over.

'This Is My Brother'

She got home on the bus exhausted —
and was not pleased to see a strange car
parked outside the cottage.

Walking in the front door, the dogs
wagged their tails, but she was shocked
to see Geoff looking thin and pale —
what on earth had happened to him?

And where was her baby?

It was only when she spied Geoff,
holding Victor, and standing behind the
man she thought at first was Geoff, that
she realised that she'd made a mistake.

'Vera, this is my brother, Tony.'

Ah yes, Geoff had mentioned he had
two brothers, and this must be one of
them. Then she remembered she'd also
been told that one of them had been a
prisoner-of-war, and by the gaunt look
of the man, and that he looked so like
Geoff, it must be him.

'Tony,' she said putting out her hand

to shake his, but at once she realised she'd made another error, because Tony's right arm was stiff and he was not able to shake hands.

'Sorry,' she muttered, and immediately she stood on tiptoe and kissed his cheek — and was rewarded with a wide smile.

'You are so alike,' Vera said smiling at the two brothers.

'People have often remarked on it,' Tony said. 'Family likenesses are extraordinary. The men in our family are all the same height, build and have the same colour eyes and hair — and your young Victor has many of these features already and is going to grow to be just the same.'

Vera held her breath — would Geoff disagree?

He did not. He just smiled fondly at his brother.

'My son,' said Geoff, 'is going to have my looks, but I hope he'll have Vera's talents.'

'I'd rather he was an engineer like

you, than a cook,' retorted Vera.

Geoff shook his head. 'The responsibility of building bridges that won't fall down is too great,' he said, 'I wouldn't wish on him the worries I've had.'

'You can have disasters when cooking too,' Vera said.

'Oh indeed, Vera, I know,' he said, pretending to be serious, 'I've suffered your overcooked dishes of macaroni pudding, and burnt buns.'

'You haven't ever been served up with food like that!' Vera glared at her husband.

Tony came between them.

'Now you two, the war is over, remember?'

He turned to kiss Vera whispering, 'My eldest brother tells me you are the greatest cook in the world.'

'I try,' Vera said modestly.

'Well, sister-in-law, how about cooking the supper, and let me be the judge?'

Tired though she was, Vera made a special effort with the supper that evening and they all enjoyed the simple but nicely prepared food.

Much to Vera's surprise they had an enjoyable evening of entertainment. Many stories the brothers exchanged about their wartime experiences — including the tale of Tony's capture and his years in a prisoner of war camp.

It did them all good to have things to talk about. And the chance for the men to discuss what they wanted to do in the future, now their war service was ended.

A New Beginning

Vera left the two brothers to go and feed her baby. She looked down at the youngest Parkington male and smiled as she kissed him then placed him back in his cot. Hearing the men still chatting downstairs, she left them to it, and went to bed.

It wasn't until she awoke the next morning that she realised Geoff was snuggled down beside her. He was still fast asleep as she rolled over and kissed him.

Of course, Tony would need the spare room, she told herself, as she got up to get her breakfast.

After that she had to catch the early bus for Lynn, because she needed to be there to supervise the cooking.

'Vera,' Geoff said coming downstairs in his pyjamas, 'best of luck with your party food — despite me teasing you yesterday, I think you are the tops, and will provide a wonderful spread for everyone to enjoy.'

He'd come from the staircase to pad over in his bare feet to give her a hug and a kiss — which surprised and delighted her.

'Now I don't want you to worry about little Victor. Tony is going to drive us to Lynn and your mother will look after him all day as we arranged.'

Vera was pleased to know her mother would be able to take care of Victor and she could concentrate on her job.

'And good luck with your fiddling,' she said grabbing her basket with the last minute things she had to take with her.

'I'm hoping the kids will be making so much noise no-one will hear the music,' he remarked.

'Go on!' retorted Vera, 'you're lucky — no-one has to eat what you do. I have to conjure up piles of party food everyone likes. Anyway, you're not that bad.'

'Neither are you.' He was teasing her she could tell, but she smiled.

'See you later.' His eyes on her made her melt and she wanted to stay with him.

But she took a deep breath.

'Here we go then!' she said marching out of the cottage.

The Country Comes Together

The VE Celebration Party was better than Vera's wildest dreams. True, some of the food turned out less than perfect, and some of the older children, wearing paper hats they'd made, were especially noisy, squealing and spilling their drinks.

Several plates got tipped over and unfortunately a few glasses and plates got broken, but overall it was a success because everyone let their hair down, and were determined to enjoy the feast — including some dogs who snapped up any food the children dropped.

'The food was delicious,' Vera heard time and time again.

Geoff's musical group played songs the children knew and could sing to, and she couldn't decide which was worse, the children's singing or the musical instruments. Anyhow, Tony was good at being an entertainer, encouraging everyone to sing, and telling a few jokes that all but the children had probably heard before, but everyone enjoyed the show and clapped heartily.

It was fun too, for Vera, when the scramble to prepare the food, and to clear the kitchen up when it was over, and she could relax.

She could find her friends, meet people and join her family.

By that time it was later in the evening and the smaller children were taken off to bed, so the adults could enjoy a glass of beer and begin to dance if they felt like it.

Mrs Carter, whose neighbour had brought her into town by car with John, and Victor, so they could join in the fun for an hour or two, told Vera that she would now take her grandson home until Vera came to fetch him.

'It doesn't matter how late you are, dear,' she said.

'But you must get to bed before long
— you'll be tired,' Vera replied.

'We'll leave the door unlocked so you
can creep in and get Victor.'

It was still wartime, but no-one feared
that their house might be broken into.

'OK, Mum. Thanks for looking after
him today.'

She and John looked at each other
and smiled.

'He's no trouble. He's such a good
baby.'

'Enjoy your evening, Vera,' said John,
'now off you go and dance the night
away — after all the work involved in
that party fare you deserve it.'

'My girls did all the work — I just
watched them work.'

John smiled broadly and said, 'Vera,
you are not the kind of person to sit on
your hands. I know you were there in
the kitchen, buzzing around, making
sure that everything they made was
going to be delicious. And so it was.
Congratulations. Geoff must be very
proud of you.'

How pleased Vera was that her mother had married John, and they were now like Darby and Joan.

How she wished she and Geoff could be the same.

It was when Vera couldn't find Geoff that she began to worry.

★　★　★

So many people were out enjoying themselves, everywhere was crowded and noisy. Hunting around, and not finding Geoff, she became convinced that the festivities might have become too much for him because he'd been used to a quiet environment since his accident.

She wondered if his brother had perhaps taken him home, but surely they would have found her and told her they were leaving the party?

Hearing dancing music being played loudly on the tannoy, so that people could hear it in the streets around the town hall, Vera approached. Looking here and there for him in the crowd, suddenly she heard . . .

'Zoooo!'

'Woops!'

A boy with outstretched arms, pretending to be a Spitfire, raced into her.

'Sorry, missus,' the boy apologised as he helped Vera back on her feet.

Her annoyance at being floored, as well as noticing her new nylons had been laddered, she still managed to hide her upset as she brushed down her dress saying, 'Try and be more careful where you are flying, young man.'

The boy's freckled face broke into a wide grin and he flew off.

Shaken, but determined not to cry on this joyous occasion, she sat down on the town hall steps to recover.

'Vera! We've been looking everywhere for you.'

Looking up she saw a group of people waving to her. Yes, and to her relief, there was Geoff, right in the middle being made a fuss of by her

British Restaurant girls. But he rose on seeing her and came up to kiss her, so that everyone clapped and cheered.

'Let's go and dance,' Geoff said taking her hand and leading her off into the crowd of dancers.

Blissful it was to be in his arms, dancing with him as they used to before he was injured.

'It's a pity young Victor isn't old enough to remember this great day,' Vera said, 'he was asleep when Mum took him back home.'

Geoff held her tightly, and she rested her head on his chest.

'He'll have a better time of it than we've had, Vera. There is only one thing he could do with.'

'What's that?'

'A sister — or a brother.'

Vera smiled.

'We'll have to see if we can manage that!' she said dreamily, knowing she had found her lover again at last.

FOLLOW YOUR HEART

Margaret Mounsdon

Marie Stanford's life is turned upside down when she is asked to house sit for her mysterious Aunt Angela, who has purchased a converted barn property in the Cotswolds. Nothing is as it seems . . . Who is the mysterious Jed Soames and why is he so interested in Maynard's? And can she trust Pierre Dubois, Aunt Angela's stepson? Until Marie can find the answers to these questions she dare not let herself follow her heart.